KARMA POLICE

Karma Police Book Two

SEAN PLATT

DAVID W. WRIGHT

STERLING & STONE

KARMA POLICE

Chapter One

Something is wrong.

I can feel it in the air, on my skin, and in my brain: static disrupting a radio signal. But it's not the hissing of meaningless noise; it's a message — one I might decipher if I could only suss out the words. But they're barely audible, lost in the real-world clamor.

Today, I'm in the body of Renaldo Vasquez. I'm twenty-five, a former drug runner turned mall security guard when I got my girlfriend, Vera, pregnant. Now I'm living the straight and narrow, or trying my best.

I began hearing the voices, like barely audible whispers, just after lunch. I was walking the food court, and at first thought some of the punk dropouts hanging around were messing with me. I moved away, far enough away that I wouldn't be able to hear them, but the sounds were still there. Then I thought maybe someone had left the public address system on and I was hearing some interference or conversation happening near the microphone. I asked one of the other guards, a big black dude named James Jones, if he could hear anything. He shook his head and asked if

I'd share whatever drugs I was obviously doing. I laughed, said I wish I was on something, and went about my rounds.

The signal died for the rest of the day, until about fifteen minutes ago when I started patrolling the parking lot. The sounds are a bit louder but still indecipherable.

Now it's 4:25 p.m., about an hour and a half before I get off.

There's an electricity in the air.

Something is about to happen.

I wish I had a gun. Unfortunately, all we get on this job are pepper spray, a baton, and a Taser. Hopefully, whatever's going to happen involves someone who isn't packing heat.

I cup my hands over my ears in an attempt to hear better. But that only increases the din of a cool breeze, gathering into the threat of a storm.

On a whim, and I'm not even sure why, I decide to cover my ears.

Now I hear it — an almost robotic voice. "Four forty-five. Red Hyundai. In front of the Nordstrom." Then the voice gives me a license plate number.

I can't believe my ears. *What* is this? My first thought is that I'm picking up on someone, maybe another guard's signal, but the voice doesn't sound like the ones on my radio. Maybe Renaldo has fillings and is picking up something from police dispatch? No, that doesn't feel right, either.

This is something else, and I can't help but feel it's tied to the mystery of whatever I am — jumping from body to body for the past year. I already know there are others like me. Maybe this is how they communicate?

I continue to cover my ears, listening to the voice, like a recording, repeating the message.

I look around. Nordstrom is on the other side of the

mall. I glance at my watch: *4:30 p.m.* I can make it if I hustle.

I run as fast as Renaldo's legs will take me. Fortunately, he's in good shape. He played soccer as a kid and ran from the police more than a few times as a teenager.

I haul ass, dodging people and cars, earning honks, the Nordstrom sign a tease in the distance.

I'm at the road dividing the lots. Forced to wait as vehicles snake in and out of the shopping mall.

Come on, come on!

I look at his watch: *4:39.* Not much time to find the Hyundai.

Traffic halts in the far lane as the lights turn red.

I run for it.

"Yo, Renaldo!" I hear behind me.

I hope it's not another one of the other guards. The last thing I need is to be followed. Whatever I'm supposed to see, it needs to be alone. This isn't some shoplifter; this is big.

I turn and see three dudes getting out of a car. The tallest is looking at me, expecting a response. I get a flash of memory, but not enough to tell me who it is, or whether he's friend or foe.

I point at Nordstrom and say the first excuse that comes to mind. "Can't stop. Gotta shit!"

Guy laughs, along with the other two. "Catchya later," he says.

I turn to see the cars still stopped in the lane, waiting for the green.

Watch says *4:40.*

Shit. Only five minutes to find the car.

The light turns green, and the cars are about to move.

I can't wait.

I launch forward, running in a space between two cars.

I make it through the first lane.

As I run into the next lane, a loud horn, squeal of tires.

I look up in time to see a black car stop. Angry dude behind the wheel looks up, yelling something I can't hear because his windows are closed and his music is screaming.

I throw up an apologetic hand, then race away.

I bolt through the bushes along the edge of the Nordstrom parking lot. *I'm here. Now where the hell is that red Hyundai?*

The parking lot is a sea of cars, at least twenty rows deep. And I don't know models well enough to distinguish between a Hyundai and a Toyota or any other similar looking vehicle, even if I were close enough to see them all better, so I focus on red cars.

Too many and not enough time.

I look at the watch.

4:44 p.m.

Instead of cars, I look for people. I assume whatever's going to happen will be initiated by a person.

What if the person is in the car? Maybe they're headed straight toward the front of Nordstrom right now?

I stop, scanning the lot for any fast-moving vehicles.

Nothing.

Shit.

Where are you?

I run straight, cutting a line through the rows, hoping something will jump out, and that in my haste I'm not heading in the wrong direction.

Suddenly, the whispers, transmission, whatever it was, stops.

In the silence, I fear I've lost whatever I was supposed to see.

Shit. I'm too late.

Panic swells in my throat as I frantically spin around, searching for something, *anything*.

Come on!

Then I see something, two aisles ahead.

A person in a dark hoodie standing beside a red car — it might be a Hyundai — looking around suspiciously as if they're about to break the window.

I drop behind a blue pickup before the person turns toward me.

I pause, catching my breath as I wait to peek around the van's corner.

Is this why I'm here? To stop someone from stealing a car? Doesn't feel like that big of a thing. I feel almost cheated. Rather than tapping into some cosmic force guiding me toward something big, I've turned into a police scanner.

Slowly, I stand, then peer around the van.

The car's still there, but the person is gone.

I look around but don't see him.

Did he get in the car?

I step forward, eyes glued to the vehicle as I make my way toward it.

Cold wind is picking up, thunder rolling in the distance.

My heart is racing. Goosebumps running up my arms, hairs standing on the back of my neck.

I hear the voices again.

I stop next to a white van, raise my hands to block the sounds of the outside world.

But the voice isn't the same.

Now it's a woman: "White van. Security guard."

My heart freezes. My throat has claws.

Footsteps behind me.

I spin around, hand on the Taser.

Too late.

Dark Hoodie is standing in front of me. But it's not a he. It's a she, a young Asian holding a gun.

Our eyes lock.

And in her eyes I see the slightest tremor of azure light. She's a Jumper! And judging from her expression, she recognizes that I am, too.

She raises her gun. "You're not stopping me."

"Stopping you from what?"

I move my hand from my belt, away from the Taser, letting her know I'm not a threat.

She looks me up and down, takes a step closer, though not close enough for me to try wresting the gun away, even *if* I'm fast enough.

"Don't play dumb. You're not saving him. He needs to die."

"I'm serious. I don't know what's going on. I heard the voices and came here."

Her eyes widen as she takes another step toward me.

"Wait, you're not one of them?"

She reaches out and touches my skin. A rush of images floods my mind, too fast to decipher.

Her jaw drops.

"Oh, my God. It's ... *you.*"

I wait to see if she'll offer a name — I'm not about to tell her.

She lowers the gun. "They've been looking for you."

Lightning cracks, blinding white accompanied by the boom of thunder.

"*Who* is looking for me? I can't remember anything."

"Nothing?"

"No. I only know I'm waking up in a different body every day or so, but I can't remember anything before a year ago."

She's not freaking out or calling me crazy. It feels like such a relief. Finally, someone I can talk to, and maybe get some answers from.

"So, you're saying you have no memories at all? None?"

I could tell her that I do have one memory, my name. But something — maybe the gun — tells me not to trust her just yet.

I shake my head. "None."

She laughs. I'm still not sure if she's an enemy.

"I'll tell you more, but first I need you to go. I have a job to do."

"What kind of job?" I ask, looking at the gun.

"You really don't remember?"

I shake my head.

"Let's just say I need to take care of someone. Call it *preventative measures.*"

Suddenly, the sound of footsteps to our left.

"Put the gun down!"

We both turn to see James standing there, gun — where he got it from I don't know — in hand, aimed at the woman.

"Shit," she says.

Before James can react, she fires two shots to his head.

I scream, "What the fuck?"

She looks at me. "Great, now I've gotta delay the job."

"What are you talking about?"

She raises the gun, says, "Sorry, no hard feelings," and fires.

Chapter Two

I WAKE UP GASPING, grateful to be alive, even if in another body.

But I've let another person die.

Not "a person." He has a name — Renaldo Vasquez!

He'd fought so hard to change his life, to be something more than the wretched person he had been before. It was tough, but he was on the right path.

But *I* screwed it up.

Maybe he's not dead. I don't know for certain. Maybe he's recovering in the hospital.

When I get up, I'll find a computer and search for his name, see if he pops up in a news story that'll tell me if he lived.

But I don't want to get up yet.

I need to lie here for a while and make sense of yesterday.

Who was that woman? How did she know me? And who was she trying to kill?

And why the hell did she shoot me?

But I can't think now. It feels like a marching band has

stomped across my body, echoes of their drums reverberating double time inside my skull.

In other words, I feel like absolute hell, waking up, yet again, in the body of someone who partied too hard the night before. I'm left to suffer the fog of confusion, struggling to find even the slightest motivation to drag this wasted body out of bed.

Today I'm in a forty-three-year-old man named Frank Miller, a warehouse worker at a mall department store, a job he hates almost as much as he loathes his sobriety. A job he's due to be at — I look at the clock: *7:15 a.m.* — in just over an hour. I live on Baker Street, a small cul-de-sac in the 'burbs, where the block's other nine houses are all newer and nicer than mine. But we're in a good area, even if Frank doesn't know a single neighbor.

I'm alone in bed, though I didn't go to sleep that way. Frank lives with his girlfriend, Stacy — a bookkeeper at a local auto parts distributor. She must be up, maybe getting her son ready for school.

I drag myself to the bathroom, flick on the light, and look at the grizzled face. He's thin, acne-scarred with severe blue eyes and long, straggly brown hair. He reminds me of a drug dealer or a roadie who parties more often than not.

I try to access last night's memories, but everything's fuzzy. Two toxic emotions are still stirring through his brain — rage and shame.

What did you do, Frank Miller?

I step into the shower and turn the hot water on, waiting for the heat to coax some hidden reserve of energy that will help me get through this day. From Frank's memories, I can tell that his job is long hours of back-breaking work. I'm not sure why a guy who has a job like that would pollute his body so much the night before. How does he get through the day?

I try going over yesterday's details but can hardly wade through Frank's chaotic emotions — so much fear and anger.

❧

IN THE YEAR I've spent jumping from body to body, forced to live other people's days, I've never experienced residual emotions this strong. Usually, there'll be a slight flavor of my host left behind. If they have a great sense of humor, I'll find myself more easily laughing at things; if they're introverted, I'll find myself a bit more withdrawn; and if they're an asshole, I'll find my temper is shorter than usual. But Frank's emotions are overriding my every instinct.

This might be easier if I could remember my personality, find some anchor to drop and ride out this storm. But other than the name, Ella, I have no memories of *my life*, nothing to guide me in *how to be* on any given day.

But Frank's rage makes me afraid of how I'll behave around others. How much of *him* will follow me into the day?

I dry off and get dressed.

I head toward the small, dark kitchen where morning sun is barely making a dent through open drapes in the window above the sink. The kitchen reeks of poverty and despair: cluttered countertops, water-stained ceiling, ripped and faded wallpaper, appliances that are fifteen years past their prime, and a sink overflowing with dirty dishes. All of it annoys me, makes my skin itch.

A twelve-year-old boy with dark hair hanging in his eyes is sitting at the small kitchen table, eating a bowl of

Fruit Loops. Tommy, Stacy's pussy son from her convict ex-boyfriend.

I try to shake Frank's feelings out of my mind. He can't stand the kid. Sees him as an impediment to his relationship with Tommy's mom.

I feel horrible for the boy.

"Good morning," I say, wondering about Frank's typical greeting.

"Good morning," he mumbles, not looking up, eyes fixed to his bowl as if he's searching for Toucan-Fucking-Sam at the bottom. I wonder if he's a moody brat, or merely hates his mom's boyfriend.

I see a newspaper sitting across from the kid — Frank's spot. An empty glass is facedown.

I pick it up.

"Where's your mom?"

I head to the fridge looking for something to wet my dry mouth.

"She went to get you some eggs."

"Okay," I say, annoyed, though I don't know why. There's a part of me, or Frank, that feels suspicious.

Went to get me eggs? Yeah, right, she's out fucking around.

I shake my head, trying to swim against the tide of jealousy and doubt that seem to anchor Frank in misery.

I survey the fridge's sad array of contents: a pitcher of Kool-Aid; a half-gallon carton of milk, almost empty, likely used by Tommy; an almost-empty container of bologna, a few bowls with leftovers covered in foil; and three cans of Old Milwaukee beer.

Instinctually, Frank's hand reaches for a beer, but I pull back, grab the milk, and slam the fridge shut harder than I intend to.

I go to the cupboard, pull out a plastic cup, and pour the remaining milk inside, annoyed that the kid's bowl is practically overflowing, way more than he needs for his tiny bit of cereal, while all I get is a fucking sip.

I hate feeling this way. Frank's anger taints my every thought. A filter is turning things I might normally notice without annoyance into tiny bombs threatening to set me off.

I desperately want to be out of this body.

I sit down.

I look at Tommy, hair hanging over his eyes as he slowly lifts a spoon into his mouth, careful not to meet my eyes.

I drink the milk in one swallow. A part of me wants to slam down the cup, let him know it's empty, thanks to his being a selfish little shit.

I fight the rage and open the paper, the *Plymouth Creek Herald.*

So, I'm in Plymouth Creek, California. While it's on the West Coast, just like every other place I've been in my body jumping journey, I don't think I've been here yet.

I skip past the local news and head straight to the op-eds in the back, to get the town's flavor, or at least the people this particular paper represents. Are they liberal? Conservative?

I'm not even sure what *I* am.

Can't tell what Frank is, either. He hates all politicians, but also just about every ethnicity that isn't white. He hates rich people most of all. Blames them for every shitty thing that's happened in his crappy little life.

There's a part of me that would love to stay in someone like Frank for a while, to help them out, to show them that life isn't that bad. Mostly it's what you make of it. Show them that his hate is pointless and mostly harms him more than others. He needs a change of perspective. From the bits of memories I can sift through in the haze, he had a rough childhood, abusive parents, got picked on. An outcast as one of the only white boys in a mostly black and Latino neighborhood. A perfect recipe for the monster he's become. But even if I could stay inside him for weeks or months until I could finally show Frank that he can turn things around, that everyone else isn't the enemy, what would happen when he woke up back in his body? How quickly would he revert to old rage and familiar habits? How much could I correct his hardwiring in just a few —

A loud crash pulls me from my thoughts.

I practically leap out of my seat.

Tommy is standing there staring horrified at his bowl of cereal, still spinning on the floor.

He throws his hands over his face and squeezes his eyes shut. The flinch. You can tell so much from a flinch. And that's when I see it — the bruises on his left cheek.

Frank did that.

Oh, God.

"I'm sorry," he bawls, "I know I'm supposed to be finished with breakfast before you wake up. I was just hurrying to the sink so I could get out of your hair."

My heart breaks as Tommy runs to the counter, tears streaming down his face. He drops to the floor, trying to mop up the milk and Fruit Loops.

"It's okay," I say, putting a hand on his shoulder.

Another flinch.

I pull my hand back.

God, I want to be out of this body.

The front door opens. A short, slightly heavyset woman in her early thirties comes in holding a bag. Stacy.

She sees Tommy on the floor, cleaning.

"What happened?"

She looks at me, then quickly looks away, eyes to her son.

"Nothing. He dropped his cereal bowl. No big deal."

Is she scared of Frank too?

Does she know that Frank hit Tommy last night?

I figure she has to know.

Did she try to stop him?

No.

I can tell from her defeated body language as she enters the kitchen, sets the bags on the table, and grabs paper towels to help clean the mess that she likely didn't try to stop him.

"Go ahead, and get ready for school, honey," she says to Tommy, who is wiping tears from his eyes.

"Okay."

"Here, I'll get it," I say, trying to be helpful.

"No, I've got it. You need to get to work."

I look at the clock, not sure how long it takes to drive to the mall, but I go ahead and take the opportunity to leave.

"Okay, I'll see you later," I say, wanting to offer Stacy a kiss, a hug, a peck on the cheek, or something. But she's so busy cleaning up and actively not meeting my eyes that I don't get the chance.

They're both scared of Frank.

I hate this man.

I let his memories guide me to where he keeps his wallet and keys, on a shelf next to the front door, then I say, "See you later."

"Bye," she says, still wiping the floor.

I step outside and stop dead in my tracks. There are two cars. One is Stacy's battered white Ford Focus. And then there's the other.

Frank's car.

The same Red Hyundai that the woman was waiting at yesterday. I stagger back, losing my balance with the realization that Frank was her target. He was the one she needed to kill. And I interfered.

I'm trembling. Barely able to move, I force myself to the car.

I get in, keys shaking in my hand, fumbling until I find the right one and key the ignition.

Why was she trying to kill Frank?

And why am I now in his body?

And perhaps the most relevant question: Will she return, as the same woman or someone else? Someone I'll never see coming?

I back out of the driveway, turn the car around, and leave the cul-de-sac, heading to work. My head is spinning in too many different directions, trying to sort through Frank's few memories, searching for some clue as to why he's an assassin's target. Best I can tell, he's a nobody loser stuck in a dead-end job, so messed up he can't keep from hurting the only woman that's probably ever loved him, or her kid.

But there are a ton of guys like that in the world. What makes Frank so special that someone — let alone a fellow Jumper — is trying to kill him?

I look in the rearview, into Frank's eyes, searching for answers. I'm not seeing them if they're there.

I hit the freeway and traffic.

I feel myself wanting to hit the steering wheel, to curse, remnants of Frank's personality so etched into his body that they're almost on autopilot. I've never felt so out of control.

I wonder if a part of Frank is still in here with me. I was feeling remnants of Lara, Yvonne, and Vinnie a week or so ago. In the three bodies I've been in since saving Allie, none of my hosts had stayed behind. Lara and the others faded more from my memory with every new day.

Is Frank still inside his body somehow? If so, why? If not, then how is so much of his temper affecting me? Maybe it has to do with his drunken state. Maybe there is some blurring of emotions that carries into the morning. I'm not sure that makes any sense in any scientific way, but then again, I'm not a scientist. At least I don't think so. I'm just a traveler learning the rules as I go.

I hit the radio's ON button and am immediately greeted with a political talk show with some blowhard talking about how they want to "take America back to the good ol' days."

I turn it back off.

As I sit in traffic molasses, I wait for more of Frank's memories to fill in some blanks.

Why does Stacy stay with him? Maybe she's just as awful as he is. Whatever Frank feels about her, I'm not sensing much. Does he love her? Is he using her? I don't get the feeling that she makes a lot of money, but there are other reasons people use one another. Maybe she validates him in some way. Or maybe he needs someone to abuse, and she doesn't have the self-worth to walk away.

I can't imagine she's so broken that she'd let him harm her child. Maybe this was a one-time thing. Maybe he's never hit Tommy before and spent half the night apologizing before passing out blind drunk. I don't know. And even if I did, what can I do?

I'm here for one, maybe two days.

Then I realize: maybe I'm here to help Frank keep his appointment with death.

FRANK'S JOB isn't just dull. It's also so physically demanding that I've almost stopped thinking about the fact that a killer may be lurking behind any of the faces I see through the morning.

The only reminder of the weirdness comes in the small talk, coworkers, both on the sales floor and in the warehouse, commenting in whispers about the two security guards killed yesterday. A few people ask me what I think. I echo their sentiments. *It's tragic. How can that happen here?* The usual stuff people say in an aftermath. We haven't yet reached Phase Two of Tragedies, where people wonder what role the victims played in their own murder. *Surely,* this was a drug deal gone bad or something.

I'm almost thankful when deliveries begin to come in, and we're split up to unpack several large pallets of merchandise, checking them against bills of lading, then bringing them to assigned spots on the towering metal shelves.

There are three other workers today, down one who called in sick. There's a Puerto Rican guy named Angel, in his early twenties. He calls everyone boss, but beyond that has little to say. Marge is a heavyset leather-faced woman in her early fifties who smells like a cigarette factory. She curses like a sailor but seems otherwise friendly enough. Then there's Stan.

Stan is a short, balding, skinny guy in his late thirties. He spends half the morning barking orders like he's vying for first place in an Asshole Match, and the other half walking the department store floor, doing God only knows what. Everyone seems to agree that they'd rather have him out of the warehouse, even if it means more work for us.

At eleven o'clock, my back is aching, and my stomach is growling something fierce. Fortunately, it's also time for my first break, a fifteen-minute reprieve from the grind.

I head to the break room upstairs. It's a fairly large space that doubles as the morning meeting room where we had a lame morale-boosting pep talk. Judging from the morning's fatigued faces, it failed to do its job. There are twenty or so tables, and plenty of bright orange plastic molded chairs with metal legs just starting to rust. Lockers surround the room, paint peeling. The TV is in front, between the two restrooms.

There is also a pair of vending machines and a small kitchen area.

Stomach growling, I head to the machines, deciding I'll get a Coke and some chips. I reach into my wallet to find a couple of crumpled bills.

Of course, the machines won't take them.

I vent a muffled grunt, not wanting to draw attention from the two saleswomen sitting together and chatting over coffee.

I turn to the women, hoping Frank's memories will give me a name to work with. But he doesn't know their names.

"Excuse me," I say, "would either of you happen to have change for two dollar bills?"

One of the women looks in her purse, then gives me an apologetic look, "No. Sorry."

The other one isn't carrying a purse. She shrugs.

Great.

I head back downstairs, figuring I'll ask one of the other warehouse employees.

I'm about five minutes into my break when I run into Angel.

"Hey, man, you got change for two dollars?"

He pats his pockets, "Sorry, boss, I don't carry change. I dump that shit into my daughter's piggy bank as soon as I get it."

"Okay, thanks," I say.

I see Stan approaching, heading toward us, likely on his

way back out into the store through the double doors behind me.

"Hey, Mr. Phillips, do you happen to have change for two bucks?"

He looks at me, ignoring my question, then points toward the loading bays. "Hey, I need you to check in a vendor."

"Uh, I'm still on break."

"Well, now you're not." He gives me his asshole's smile then walks away.

I glare at the back of his shiny dome, watching him slip through the double doors, wondering why the hell he didn't ask Angel or Marge to check the shipment in. They're both still putting away stuff from this morning, but it's not like there's a rush to finish. They could easily be pulled away. Hell, *Stan* could've done it himself.

I head back to the bay and check in the vendor, which takes about fifteen minutes. I check off the bill of lading then bring a copy to the boss's office, drop it in a box, and head back to the break room to resume my interrupted respite, hoping someone will have change.

A heavyset cashier with dark circles under his eyes has change for a buck, but not two. I thank him, then head to the soda machine for a Coke. The combination of sugar and caffeine should help me make it until lunch.

I'm sitting at a table alone near the rear, watching five employees glued to a twenty-four-hour news channel broadcasting coverage of "another senseless shooting." One of the *experts* points out that gun laws won't change things like this from happening, and, in fact, there's a good chance that the victims knew their killer.

Ah, cue Phase Two — blame the victims.

If only these smug bastards knew the truth. Not that it would change an argument to restrict gun sales. Hell, if these people knew that there are people jumping from body to body and that literally anybody could be a killer, even your family, they'd advocate guns for everyone.

I can already hear the radio advertisements.

Yes, your wife says *she loves you, but can you* really *trust her? What if she's a Jumper? Shouldn't you be prepared? Arm yourself today!*

I'm surprised to have such a visceral reaction to the pro-gun expert on TV. I don't know if it has something to do with my past, Frank's, or maybe the number of guns I've had aimed at me recently.

I'm nearly done with my Coke when Stan enters the break room.

"What are you doing?" he asks, face red.

"Finishing my break."

"Your break is from eleven to eleven fifteen. It's," he glances at a clock on the wall, "eleven twenty-one."

"I can see that. But, if you recall, you pulled me off my break to check in that vendor. Now, I'm finishing that break."

"Did I *tell you* that you could resume your break? No. I said your break was over. That means it's over. And you just left the pallet sitting there. You need to put it away."

I'm not sure what it is, the way he's talking down to me, his scrunchy rat-like face, or Frank's lingering hate for humanity, but I say something I don't quite mean to say, yet am unable to stop it from leaving my mouth.

"I've got four minutes of my break left. I'll put it away then."

"What did you say?"

Stan gets right in front of me, staring down like he's planning to hit me. A part of me would love it if he tried. Well, I'm not sure if it's a part of me or a part of Frank. Either way, I do my best *not* to push the violence.

"Lemme just finish this Coke, and I'll do it."

"Out," he says.

"Excuse me?"

"I said out. You're fired."

"Fired? For taking the break I'm allowed to take? You pulled me off. I'm just getting my fifteen minutes."

"Hey, you wanna relax so much, go home, relax all you want, and maybe think about your shitty attitude."

I stand. The chair scrapes the floor and draws everyone's eyes.

Stan is about a foot shorter than Frank, but he's not backing down. He glares up at me as if waiting for me to hit him, fists balled at his side.

There's history here, and hell, maybe Frank has earned his boss's ire before now. But still, firing him over this is stupid.

My heart is racing. A hot wave is washing over me.

I barely keep my rage from erupting.

I smile, trying to pull this back from the edge. I don't want to get Frank fired because of *my* mouth.

"Listen, I'm sorry. I missed breakfast and needed something to keep me going. I'll take care of that pallet now."

Stan stares at me, not responding. The dead look in his eyes is unnerving.

"Is that okay?"

Finally, he responds. "No. I want you to take your Coke, and get the hell out of here. Don't come back."

He presses his finger into my chest to illustrate his point.

I lose it.

I grab his finger, pull it, and his hand, behind his back, then shove him forward, slamming Stan's face into the lockers.

"Don't you fucking touch me!" I yell.

He cries out, his face squished against the metal, "Let go!"

But I don't want to let go. I want to break his fingers, then sit back down and finish my Coke with a smile.

Instead, I let go and back away a few steps.

He turns to me, brow furrowed, face red with embarrassment, hands straightening his clothes, though I didn't ruffle them.

"You ever come back on this property, I will have your ass arrested. Now get out!"

I want to say something, but I'll only make things worse.

So I leave, wondering what the hell just happened.

THIS ISN'T RIGHT. I'm not supposed to interfere in my host's life, let alone get him fired from his job.

I'm sitting in Frank's car, still in the parking lot, staring at the steering wheel and wondering what to do.

Should I go back and apologize, beg for Frank's job? Or should I go home and get drunk? I know what Frank would do. But how can I help?

I'm still pissed and don't want to blow up on anybody, so I head for home, hoping that no one is there.

I'M SITTING at Frank's kitchen table, trying to think of the best way to deal with this situation. When he wakes up tomorrow, assuming I'm out of his body and not stuck for a second day of hell, he'll probably wonder how he lost his job. From what I know, he'll have a few memories that I've left behind, and his brain will fill in the gaps to make sense of what little he has. But this feels like an awful lot of white space to color.

How the hell do I keep him from losing his shit? From going to the store and causing a scene?

I start searching through the classifieds, circling jobs that look like possibilities for someone with Frank's limited skill set, education, and people skills.

The doorbell rings.

I get up and look outside to see the mail truck sitting at the end of the driveway.

I open the door to a short, bald mailman holding a pad in both hands.

Where's the package I'm supposed to sign for?

No sooner do I think this then he drops the pad, wielding a blade cutter in his left hand.

He lunges at me.

My instincts kick in, and I dodge to the left then grab his right arm to twist it back behind his back. But something else happens when we touch.

Another flood of incoherent memories.

It's the Jumper!

I let go.

Our eyes meet.

"You?" he says, stepping back, making no move to swipe again. "Why are you here, again?"

"Why are you trying to kill him?"

"You know … oh wait, you don't … we don't know the whys. We only know that the job must be done. He's a bad guy, or he wouldn't be on The List."

"What do you mean *we?* Are you some kind of assassin?"

He nods.

"Was I?"

He stares at me, not confirming or denying.

"I have a job to do. A job that you've now prevented twice."

He slides the blade into his pocket, bends over to recover the pad, apparently feeling safe that I won't attack him. Then he turns around and heads back to his truck.

"Wait," I say, "you're giving up?"

"I can't kill him when one of us is in the body."

"Wait. I need to know more. I need answers. Was I an assassin?"

The Jumper turns back to me, shaking his head. "Sorry. I can't."

"What do you mean you *can't?*"

"Just trust me, okay. You're better off not knowing. There's a reason you don't remember anything, so stop trying. And please, try not to mess with my job tomorrow."

He turns and heads to his mail truck.

Nothing I can say will bring him back.

I PACE THE KITCHEN, frustrated, trying to avoid alcohol's siren song from the fridge.

The urge to drink is like an itch that needs scratching, but I'm afraid to start in this body. It's already full of a toxic brew of rage and chaos. I don't want to add anything volatile. It's not that I think I'd lose control and hit Tommy or Stacy, but I don't want to do anything that makes controlling this body more difficult than it already is. I'm pushing one of those shopping carts with an errant wheel, and it's a struggle just to keep it straight.

I decide to lie down in his bedroom and watch some TV. I flip around until I stop on a sitcom I've never seen, figuring it'll relax me. With any luck, I'll fall asleep and wake up tomorrow far away from Frank and the assassin.

I try to focus on the show, but my mind keeps drifting back to Frank and the Jumper attempting to kill him. But not just the Jumper, but what the Jumper had said.

"We don't know the whys. All we know is that the job needs to be done. He must be a bad guy, or he wouldn't be on The List."

Who is *we?* And what is *The List?*

I remember the voices I'd heard while in Renaldo's body, leading me to the Hyundai. Voices that sounded like communications, instructions for the assassin. But it wasn't just her instructions. Someone, another voice, was leading me to the car as well. And the assassin knows me, or at least *of* me, yet is warning me not to dig deeper.

What's happening here? Was I part of some body jumping assassin's guild or something? If so, what happened? How did I get separated from them, and why don't I remember anything?

I can't imagine killing anyone. Yes, I did a couple of weeks ago, but that was different. I was fighting to protect myself, and to save Allie Martin from the serial killer. But killing someone on a *list?* The thought makes me sick to my stomach.

Frank's a terrible guy, but does he deserve to die? I'm not picking up on any memories, other than flashes from last night's incident. Yes, he hit Tommy, but he feels ashamed. I can't imagine that was routine.

How could some group determine he needs to die for his sins?

Who are these Jumpers? And are they *all* assassins?

A chill runs through me. Before now, I thought, or at least hoped, that I'd someday have a normal life. I'd return to *my body* — wherever it is — and resume *my life.*

But what if I don't have a body or a life of my own?

What if this is forever?

<h1 style="text-align:center">Chapter Three</h1>

I WAKE to an alarm clock's angry buzz.

I reach out and hit the snooze button. This body is exhausted. And young. I've only woken up in a child host a few times, so far as I can remember, and am always surprised by how much energy I have in their bodies. Even when the kids are tired, they're never depleted like older bodies.

I open my eyes, see that the clock reads, *6:30 a.m.* My room is dark, so I turn on the lamp next to me, illuminating blue walls covered in Seattle Seahawks posters and Mariners pennants. The floor is littered with clothes, books, and a few thousand Lego pieces.

I make my way out the door to the bathroom, waiting for my host's brain to fill in the details: who I am, which family and friends will I be forced to navigate while trying my best to screw the kid's day.

I step into the hallway and freeze.

Oh, my God. I'm in Tommy's body.

I'm back in Frank's life.

Why?

26

I stumble back into the bedroom, heart racing, trying to catch my breath. This is horrible. Why do I keep jumping into lives in this guy's circle? If I'm not an assassin, then what am I doing here? And who the hell is making this happen?

Why did I let the assassin go?

I should've chased him, forced him to answer. Who is he to tell me not to dig into my life's big mystery?

I remember the note the other Jumper had left with the psychic.

~

STOP SEARCHING.
> *You won't like what you find.*
> *Better to forget and let go.*
> *Only then can you live again.*

~

COULD that have been the assassin, too? And if so, who was he (or she) targeting? Did I inadvertently get Lara Spencer killed and Allie Martin kidnapped by botching an assassination attempt on Alexander Bova?

A knock on the door shakes me from my thoughts. Tommy's mom opens the door and eyes me. "You gonna get ready?"

"Yeah," I say, looking up at her and seeing two things at once — how much she loves her son, and how incredibly tired she is. Though there's a light in her eyes, there are also dark circles. I wonder how many sleepless nights Frank has cost her.

"Okay, I'm making breakfast so we can eat before Frank wakes up."

I nod, head to the shower, wash up, and return to my bedroom.

Tommy's closet offers little. Most of the clothes are hand-me-downs from Stacy's friends, which means they're either in need of repair, not quite the right size, or several years out of style. I can feel Tommy's shame as I consider my choices. I pick jeans and a red tee with a silhouette of a skateboarder, which looks like it might be the closest thing to in style. Not that I would know what's in style with teen boys. The few times I've been kids, I've either been younger or a girl, and typically the girls have had something stylish to wear. Poor Tommy is in need of a makeover, or maybe some money to get his own clothes.

Once I'm dressed, I head out to the kitchen where Mom waits with two plates of scrambled eggs and toast, along with two glasses of milk. Napkins, salt, pepper, ketchup, and Tabasco fill the center of the table, alongside a tiny vase with a yellow flower that looks like Tommy's mom might have picked it from the garden.

Though they don't have much money, I can tell that Stacy tries her best to make things pleasant for Tommy.

"Smells good," I say, taking a seat across from her.

"Thanks." She's looking down at her phone, scrolling through messages or email. I'm not sure if they're work-related or she's just catching up on personal email. Either way, I'm grateful for the silence. I don't know what sorts of things Tommy usually talks about, or if he's even particularly talkative. He didn't seem so yesterday, but that was how Frank saw him. I don't know his mother's perception and don't want to screw it up by acting out of character. Defaulting to quiet is best. A bit moody seems like a safe bet for most kids his age.

I take a drink of milk and flash back to yesterday. I hope she left enough food for Frank. I chew my eggs, searching Tommy's memories to figure out what he does in the time between these early breakfasts and when he leaves to catch the school bus. Usually, he goes back to his room and either reads or draws pictures in his spiral notebooks. While he doesn't consider himself an artist yet, Tommy loves drawing his own comics — even if he's their only reader.

Stacy quickly answers her buzzing phone.

"Hey, hold on a sec."

She looks at me, raises a finger to indicate she'll be back in a second, then heads out of the kitchen, through the back door, out to the porch. She walks away, putting as much distance between herself and the house as she can.

I wonder who she's talking to that she doesn't want me to hear. Or maybe it's Frank's ears she's avoiding.

It's still dark outside, so I can barely see her. She sees me watching, and turns away as if I might read her lips. Now I'm more curious.

I turn back to my plate and finish the eggs. I grab a piece of buttered toast and take a bite. Unfortunately, it's already cold. I keep eating; I'm hungry and don't want to insult Stacy, who goes through the effort of waking up early to have breakfast with her son. I'm not sure if Tommy appreciates the effort, or even recognizes it, but I do. I've been in enough homes to know the rarity of parents sharing breakfast, let alone any meal, with their child.

The door slides open behind me. I resist the urge to turn back, even though I'd love to see her reaction to Tommy's gaze — if it'll give away details. Was she talking with a friend to bitch about Frank? I don't know what happened after I dozed off in the afternoon and left his body. Did he sleep through the night, or did he wake up? He couldn't have been in a good mood and was more likely confused, maybe trying to figure out why he'd been fired. As curious as I am to see what he remembers from the day a stranger claimed his body, I don't want to be around for the fallout.

If he did wake up last night, I'm getting nothing from Tommy to tell me.

Stacy sits back down across from me, puts the phone on the table, eyes on her plate as she forks the eggs and takes a bite. They've gotta be cold by now, but she doesn't flinch as she swallows.

I wait for her to look at me.

When she finally does, I expect her to say something about who she was on the phone with, even though it was obviously private.

She looks at me, head tilted. "You okay?"

"Why?"

"You're eating eggs without ketchup!"

"Oh," I say, feeling exposed, "wasn't in the mood, I guess."

She gets up, puts a hand on my head. "Well, you don't have a fever." She withdraws her hand, then gives me this intense look. "Who are you, and what have you done to my son?"

She stares at me.

Oh, shit, I'm busted. How? By not eating ketchup?

My heart is racing, and I'm sure my face looks terrified.

She picks up a salt shaker, aims it like a gun. "Get out of my son, alien pod person!"

She bursts out laughing and returns the shaker to the table.

I sigh with relief.

"You're such a dork, Mom." Echoes of Tommy saying similar things stir in my head.

"Dorks are the new cool," she says, tousling my hair. "And besides, I thought you were proud to be a dork."

More flashes of memory — Stacy and Tommy sitting at this very table over the years, playing board games and cards, reading comics together. They used to have lots of fun before Frank came into the picture last year.

"Proud to be a geek, Mom, not a dork. There is a distinction."

"Hey, I like all the same things you like. And I liked most of them long before you were born. If I'm a dork, then you are too."

"Fair enough," I say with a smile.

She brushes the hair from my face and looks into my eyes.

"Ah, there's the smile I was looking for."

She's smiling, too. It feels good to see her happy. I get the feeling it's not something Tommy sees a lot of these days.

Frank steps into the kitchen, coughing loudly, looking like he just woke up from an eighteen-hour hibernation.

"Okay, who drugged me?"

I'm not sure if he's serious. His eyes are half-closed, his hair a mess, and he's still wearing the clothes he, or I, wore to work yesterday.

"Wow, you slept long," Stacy says, immediately taking her plate from the table, even though she's not finished eating.

She looks at me. Her expression tells me to stand and give the lord his space.

After putting her plate in the sink, she grabs a newspaper from the counter and hands it to him. He grabs it, shuffling past us before sitting in the chair where Stacy had been sitting just moments earlier. She goes to the oven and opens it, then pulls a plate she'd been keeping warm. She brings it over to him: eggs, toast, and bacon.

That bastard gets bacon?

I get up and bring my leftovers to the trash, scraping the remaining toast into the can. Then I bring my plate to the sink and place it, along with the fork, on top of Mom's.

I stand at the sink, hoping to hear Frank say something that might tell me what he remembers, but after a moment, I feel super-obvious and go to my room.

Fortunately, the house is small, and only one story, so even though I'm on the other side, standing in my bedroom's open doorway, I can hear Frank as he starts to talk.

At first, I don't hear what he says, but his second sentence is crystal clear. "Seriously, did you drug me?"

"What are you talking about?"

"I dunno, I feel all fuzzy. And I'm pretty sure I was fired yesterday."

"Fired?"

"Yeah, but I barely remember what happened."

"No, I didn't *drug you*," Stacy says, sounding offended, but not like she hasn't had to deal with wild accusations before. "Maybe you were … "

She either doesn't finish the allegation or says it quietly so I can't hear it, or to keep him from being offended.

"I wasn't fucking drunk!"

"I wasn't gonna say that. I was going to say maybe you've come down with something. Do you have a fever?"

I can't see her, but I'm imagining Stacy putting a hand on his head as she'd done with me.

"Hmm, don't feel warm. Maybe you should go to the clinic?"

"I'm not going to the clinic," he says, annoyed.

"So, what do you remember?"

Silence.

Suddenly, I hear footsteps.

I scramble, closing the door, making sure not to make a sound, then hop onto my bed, grabbing a book off my nightstand — a tattered old paperback of Stephen King's *Skeleton Crew* with a toy monkey on the cover.

The door opens, and I look up from the book to see Frank standing in the doorway, brows furrowed with suspicion. "Were you listenin' to us?"

"No," I say, making my eyes wide and hopefully innocent. "I'm reading."

He looks me up and down, and I try not to think about how weird it is to have this person whose body I was in yesterday staring right at me. I can almost feel his thoughts as if he can sense that I — not Tommy — had recently invaded him.

Frank says nothing then closes the door.

I breathe my second relieved sigh and try to read enough to move my mind from the disappointment of no longer being able to eavesdrop.

I LEAVE the house with Mom. She says, "Good luck" to Frank.

After she closes and locks the door, I ask what happened.

"Frank's not feeling well. He lost his job yesterday and isn't sure what happened, so he's going into work to see if he can't fix things."

I stay quiet, calculating his odds of getting his job back. I'm hoping he can, and not just because it's my fault he lost it. No, the main reason is so he's not home. Too much

Frank won't be good for anyone. The quicker he lands on his feet, the safer their household will be.

Mom looks at me. "I know what you're thinking. That he got drunk again."

I'll let her continue. Not like I'm going to tell her what I'm *really* thinking.

"You should give him a chance. He's not a bad guy."

"Really?" I say, pointing my bruised cheek. "Do *good guys* hit kids?"

I hit a nerve. Her eyes are watering, and she looks torn between protecting her son and standing by a man she loves for reasons I — and maybe even *she* — can't quite comprehend.

"I know. He shouldn't have hit you. He said it was an accident and apologized. I told him if he ever did it again, that's it. It's over."

"He didn't apologize to me," I say, feeling Tommy's resentment bubbling up.

I get a flash. This may be the first time he's hit Tommy, but he's had other *accidents* in the past. He's hit Stacy a number of times, and yet she stays.

"I don't care about him hitting me. I don't want him ever to hit *you* again. Why do you stay with him?"

"You wouldn't understand." She grabs a tissue from her pocket and blows her nose, fighting hard to stop the tears.

I hate upsetting her like this. I can tell how much she cares for Tommy. It's clear in her eyes. I saw it in how quickly she rushed to help clean the spilled milk. I can hear it in her trembling voice.

"Try me," I say.

She looks back at the house. I turn, see Frank standing in the front window, the curtain parted, staring at us.

"Can we talk about this later? How about I leave work

early and pick you up from school? We can get ice cream and talk about this whole thing. Okay?"

Her hopeful smile, the pain and love in her eyes — how can I say no?

"Okay."

She hugs me tightly. It feels good.

I'm not sure if it's the remnants of Tommy's love for his mother surging through my system, or if these are my honest responses to her warm embrace.

I have no memories of my own parents, let alone loving hugs. There's something comforting about being squeezed by someone who loves you so much — a warmth like no other sensation.

She pulls away and kisses me on the head. "I love you, Tommy."

"I love you, too, Mom."

She wipes tears from her eyes, then says, "I'll see you later."

To our right, two houses away, I see Old Man Wilbur, the neighborhood gossip sitting on his porch pretending to read the paper, when everyone knows he's spying on the street. I'm annoyed that he stole our moment, and is documenting it in his tiny round head. If I were in an older body, I might even go over and tell him to mind his own business.

Stacy gets in her car, waves back at me one more time, then heads to work.

I walk to the bus stop without looking back. I'm sure if I did, Frank would still be staring from the window.

~

~

THE BUS STOP is on a sidewalk along 112th Terrace, a fairly busy road in the subdivision.

There are twelve kids here, most sprawled along a guard rail in front of a small lake opening to backyards on either side. While all the kids are sitting within one small area, divisions within the cliques are easy enough to see if you look.

Then there are a few outcasts at the far end of the rail.

I pass by all the groups, trying to get a feel for whether any of these are Tommy's friends. Only after reaching the end do I realize he's not pals with any of these kids, including the outcasts. He's all by himself, utterly alone.

You'd think he'd have at least a friend or two, seeing as these are all neighborhood kids, but no. It's not that the kids don't like him, though I get that vibe from a few people eyeballing me as if wanting to start something. For the most part, Tommy seems invisible.

I sit on the guard rail, grab the *Skeleton Crew* book from my backpack, and read it until I hear the grinding brakes of the bus pulling up.

Somehow, I'm first in line when the bus opens its doors, and I step aboard. We're the first stop, so the bus is empty. I decide to take a seat in the back.

I focus on my book, mostly to avoid eye contact with anyone until we get to school. A few kids sit two rows ahead of me, but nobody else comes all the way back.

Do they hate Tommy that much?

I pretend to read, though it's hard to focus on the words. I can feel people staring. I hear muffled giggles, and "oohs," obviously about me, but I can't figure out what I did to draw their attention.

Did I wear some criminally out-of-fashion shirt? Do I have a booger hanging out?

I look in the window, catching enough of my reflection to check my nose.

The bus slows then settles. This next stop has double the number of kids. The doors hiss open, and there's a swell of anticipation in the air. Everyone from my stop is turning back to look at me.

What the hell is going on?

Kids from the second stop climb aboard.

All eyes turn to the newcomers, who look toward the back of the bus, at me, just like everyone else. Their eyes are wide.

I hate where this is going.

Then everyone's attention turns to the front of the bus as a tall, zit-faced muscular kid wearing a retro Iron Maiden shirt climbs aboard. He has long bright red hair and angry red eyebrows. He's glaring right at me.

Who the hell is this? And why is he giving me a death ray stare?

A name pops into my head: Evan Glassman.

Behind him, four other kids, including two girls — obviously a part of his posse — are also staring.

"Oh, shit, what is he doing?" says one of the girls, a pretty blonde cheerleader type, laughing at me.

Evan comes up to me. "What the fuck you doing in my seat, dickbag?"

"Sorry, I didn't know this was your seat," I say, looking up at Evan and his group. Everyone is watching me like Evan is going to rip me from limb to limb.

"Bullshit." Evan reaches out, grabs my book, and tosses it up the aisle.

"Hey!" I say, jumping to my feet, pissed.

I try to see where my book went, but Evan's goons are blocking my view.

His eyes widen, seemingly surprised that I stood up to him. "What?"

"Give me my book back."

Evan looks behind him, likely checking to see if the bus driver is paying attention, then turns and punches me hard right in the chest.

I fall back into the seat, gasping for air.

Laughter from his friends, who are blocking the driver's view. So long as he's quick, Evan can do whatever he wants.

He leans forward.

I'm too busy catching my breath to defend myself.

Instead of hitting me again, the bully grabs my collar, yanks me forward, and hurls me down to the floor. "Get out of our fucking seats, faggot!"

My knees feel like someone smashed them with a hammer.

The bus driver, a large black woman with large shades, calls back, "Please take your seat."

Is she talking to me? Sorry, lady, I just got *thrown* from my seat! Why isn't she calling out the junior thug and his friends who are all laughing as they take over the back two rows?

"Okay," I say, still trying to catch my breath.

I stand up, looking up the aisle, searching for a seat.

I don't see my book. One of the other kids must've grabbed it. Maybe they're gonna play keep away to torment me further. Fuckers.

I start up the aisle.

While most of the seats only have one or two kids sitting in them, and there's room for three per row, many of the kids refuse to make room or to look at me. A few even occupy more space and deny me a seat.

What the hell? Does everyone hate me?

I make my way toward the front of the bus, unable to find a seat, or anyone willing to share.

The bus driver raises her voice. "I said find a seat!"

I'm burning inside. I want to say something, but it will only sound whiney and give these assholes what they want — to see Tommy in pain.

I find a homely looking girl with giant glasses. She's from my stop. I think her name's Wendy. She doesn't look at me, but stays in her spot next to the window, not denying me space.

"Can I sit here?"

"I guess," she shrugs, even though she doesn't seem particularly happy about the arrangement. Even the outcasts hate Tommy.

I take my seat.

"Thank you," the bus driver says. I look in her big mirror to see the exasperated expression of someone with no time for bullshit.

The bus rolls forward.

I turn, looking for my book, actually Stacy's book, which she had as a teenager, and let Tommy borrow.

I don't see it.

All I see are a bunch of giggling faces and darting eyes, a bus filled with kids complicit in screwing with Tommy.

Evan is glaring at me from the back. He catches my eyes, raises a finger, and makes a slicing motion across his neck, mouthing the words, "You're dead."

Great.

We make a few more stops, and more kids board the bus. I try to ignore the giggling and whispers behind me. But I've become the highlight of everyone's morning.

I pore through Tommy's memories and realize that until now the boy has managed to fly under Evan's radar. The bully had moved to town last year and had pushed around a lot of kids since. Somehow, Tommy had avoided tripping his wire.

Until today.

Way to go, Ella.

When the bus finally gets to school, I'm torn between getting off as quickly as possible — easy since I'm in the first row — and staying behind to look for my book, which is likely lying on the floor under one of the seats. I don't want to lose Stacy's book. I can feel Tommy's sentimental attachment. Or hell, maybe I've developed an attachment. Either way, I want to feel it in my hands.

I let Wendy off, then sit and wait for everyone else to disembark.

As the procession makes its way, I keep my head down, not wanting to meet any stares or acknowledge their mocking. I hear the snide comments: *You done did it now, dork; Way to go, Tommy; Man, that was dumb.*

My heart races as the back of the bus begins to empty. I know Evan and his crew are going to say something, but with the bus driver sitting a few feet away, I figure I'm relatively safe.

Then I feel something hit the seat beside me.

I look down, it's my book, or what remains of it — cover ripped off, and several pages shredded. What's left looks like a dog has been playing with it all morning.

Evan leans toward me and whispers, "Here's your book, faggot."

Then he punches me hard on the arm.

I resist the urge to cry out and give him the satisfaction of knowing he hurt me.

I look up and meet his eyes.

Again he mouths, "You're dead."

Then he steps off the bus, and I'm all alone, fighting my tears.

~

DESPITE THE ROCKY MORNING, the school day's okay. For one, Tommy's best friend, Danny, hung out with me at lunch in the hall outside art class, commiserating over the morning's events. As lonely as I felt on the bus, having at least one friend helped me feel less alone.

Danny is a big-time geek, but not an outcast like Tommy. His brother, Dale, is on the high school football team, so he inherited some *cool by association*. Having a popular older brother also insulates him from the bullies, and has emboldened him to be quite a smart ass.

"You want me to do something?" Danny had asked.

I told him thanks but no. Just having him to share a laugh with was helpful.

Fortunately, Evan isn't in any of Tommy's classes, and when the 3:30 end-of-day bell rings, I don't have to take the bus home and receive my death sentence. I stand in the car line with Danny, who is waiting for his brother to get him.

"You sure you don't want a ride with us? I mean, you'll have to watch Dale practice, but hey, there are hot cheerleaders. *High school* cheerleaders," he says with a grin.

"Thanks, but Mom wants to talk to me about something. Plus, ice cream."

"Sorry, dude, cheerleaders beat ice cream all day every day."

I laugh. Then an awful thought finds me. What if Tommy doesn't remember this morning's incident? He needs to be on his guard tomorrow. Otherwise, Evan might blindside him. While we have ice cream, I can ask Mom to take me to school in the morning. But what about on the way home?

Maybe I can get a ride home with Danny and Dale tomorrow. It's only one day, but maybe that'll be enough for Evan to forget about Tommy and find some fresh meat to mess with.

"Hey, can I go with you tomorrow?"

"Tomorrow we're going to Grandma's after school. Maybe next time?"

"That would be awesome."

Mom's car pulls up, and I say goodbye to Danny. Time for a talk about Frank.

With any luck, the assassin found and killed him. Maybe we'll come home to an empty house. Sure, Stacy will be upset and probably scared, but they'll both be better off.

WE'RE at Johnny J's All-Night Diner, a cozy '50s-themed restaurant along a wooded highway. As we take a spot in a cherry red leather-backed booth, the gray sky opens to let loose a torrent.

"Guess we'll be here a while," Stacy says looking outside as lightning flashes.

Good, more time for the assassin to find and kill Frank.

I'd hate to get home while the assassin is there and risk either Tommy or Stacy getting killed, too.

As we wait for the waitress in her '50s poodle skirt to bring us drinks, Stacy calls Frank.

"Hey, honey, just calling to see how it went. Tommy and I are at Johnny J's if you want to join us. Give me a call. We were gonna have ice cream, but it's raining awfully hard, so I think we'll make it dinner and ice cream. Hope everything went well. Love you."

As I sit there watching Tommy's mom, a part of me wants to tell her about the bus ride. Tell her about the jerks who ripped up her *Skeleton Crew* book, and how I've now made enemies with Evan Glassman, one of the school's biggest assholes.

But I don't want to put any more on her plate than is already there. Plus, I'm not sure if this is the sort of thing that Tommy would prefer not to tell her. Who knows how she'll react, and if she might make things worse for him at school? Maybe it's best to lie low for a while, see how things shake out. Maybe the whole Evan thing will blow over. If not, maybe Danny can get Dale to intervene. This is a problem that Tommy can probably handle if he's as resourceful as I hope he is.

It's hard to tell, though, what Tommy is like. If Frank was almost ever present in his body while I was controlling it, shading every thought with his anger, Tommy is almost the opposite. I can hardly get a bead on his personality beyond how other people treat him. Well, at least in how Danny and his mother treat him, like a good kid dealing with a shitty situation.

Stacy hangs up.

"So, how was your day?" she asks.

"Okay, I guess. Yours?"

"Let's just say I'm glad I could get out early. We ought to do this more often."

"Your boss didn't mind you leaving early?"

"He's on a trip this week, so it was just Judy, and she was cool."

"Good," I say, wondering how we're going to broach the subject we're here to discuss.

The waitress brings our drinks, two cherry colas.

"Y'all decide what you want yet, or you need a few minutes?"

"We need a few minutes," I say.

I look over the menu searching for something I'm in the mood to eat. Most of the food is greasy fried stuff, but

I'm in a young, healthy body, so I can splurge. When the waitress comes back, I order a cheeseburger and fries.

Stacy orders the same, and the waitress leaves. I slide the menus behind the napkin dispenser at the edge of our table, just under the window.

Stacy makes small talk, and I endure for a while until I feel like she's delaying the topic. I cut to the chase.

"Why are you still with him? You must know that you can do better, right?"

She looks surprised. Not sure if it's too adult a comment from Tommy, or simply too blunt for her son.

"It's not like that."

"What *is* it like?"

"I love Frank. He came along at a difficult time in my life, in our lives. Your father really screwed things up. Frank saved us."

Ah, Tommy's father.

Memories fill in the details. He was a drug dealer, high end, cocaine mostly. But he wasn't like the drug dealers you see on TV. He wasn't a gangster. He didn't carry a gun, at least not that Tommy knew about. He was a car salesman who happened to make some money on the side selling narcotics. We lived in a nice house, Mom was happy, and life was good.

But then he got nabbed; no one's sure how. Then we lost nearly everything, seized by federal agents. Tommy's father was killed in a prison yard fight, which devastated both Tommy and his mom. She had to work for the first time in years, and they lived in a crappy apartment for two years before she met Frank.

He was a blue-collar guy but made decent money — and was nice, in the beginning.

"Frank didn't save us, Mom. You did. *You* got a job. *You*

worked through all of this. And we were fine before he came along."

"Fine? We had a crappy apartment in the state's worst school district. I can't even imagine you going to school there."

"So, that's the only reason you're with him, for his money, for me?"

"No, not at all. As I said, I loved, er, love him. He's been through a lot. He had a crappy childhood, and given what I know about his life, he's not nearly as bad as he could be."

"Oh, that's a relief."

She shakes her head. "Don't be like that."

"What? I'm just telling the truth. He's a jerk, and you don't need him. *We* don't need him. I'd rather live in a crack den, or on the streets, than in his house."

"He's not that bad, Tommy."

"You keep saying that. But he hits you. He freaking hits you! There's no excuse for that. I don't care how bad his childhood was."

She shakes her head. "I wish you could see him how I do. He's trying, so hard."

"Wow," I say, pointing to my bruise, "this is him *trying?* And how many times has he hit you?"

"You can't possibly understand what those two years were like before we met Frank. You're … you're too young."

"Understand what? How lonely you were?"

She doesn't say anything. Her eyes are watering, again.

I can't imagine she'd ever choose a lover over her son's safety. That doesn't seem like her. But I don't know what else could keep Stacy blinded to the danger of staying with Frank. Maybe she doesn't see him as a threat, even though his violence has escalated to Tommy. She needs to see the danger before either of them get caught in the crossfire of Frank's violent mood swings or an assassin's bullet.

"He's going to kill us," I say.

Then, of course, the waitress appears with our food.

There's an awkward silence as she sets our food on the table, just me and Stacy trading stares.

"Do you all need any — "

Mom cuts her off, "No thank you."

The waitress leaves.

Mom looks at me, eyes narrowed, and whispers, "He's *not* going to kill us. How can you even say something like that?"

"You hear about stuff like this on the news all the time. And people are always saying, 'Yeah, he was violent, but he wasn't *that bad*.' You're enabling him, Mom. He hits you; he hit me. What's next? Especially now that he lost his job?"

"What would you have me do, leave him?"

"Yeah," I say it a bit too loudly, as if it's the world's most obvious answer.

She closes her eyes, covers her face with her hands. Her weakness is infuriating.

"We can go home right now, pack our bags, and leave tonight."

"Where would we go?"

"I dunno. Don't you know anyone who could take us in until we get back on our feet?"

"Gram's in the nursing home, and I don't have any other family, at least none who are talking to me after what happened with your father."

"A coworker, I dunno. Heck, we can get a hotel room, or move to a crappy apartment. We did it before; we can do it again. Come on, Mom, we can do this."

"No." She shakes her head. "I can't leave him."

"Why? Give me one good answer."

"Because he said he'd find us and kill us if I did."
Shit.

~

FRANK IS SURPRISINGLY nice when we get home. We sit in the living room, Frank and Stacy on the couch and me in a recliner, discussing our days.

He tells us how he went to his work and his prick of a boss wouldn't give him his job back. "Screw 'em. I can do better," he says.

Stacy makes some suggestions, places she'd heard may be hiring, including a few that would offer a significant bump in pay.

The whole thing is surreal. They're talking like a happy family, no sign of either Frank's rage from yesterday or of the fact that the man has threatened Mom into imprisonment.

I'd tried to convince her to tell the police, but she's too scared. Stacy explained how no restraining order in the world could protect her if Frank were determined enough to hunt her down. Then I'd suggested we go into hiding, but she said it's not feasible. At least not now.

As we sit in the living room, I find myself starting at the television, Frank has it on ESPN, but sports are the last thing on my mind. I'm wondering why the assassin didn't return to finish the job. Had he, or she, seen that I was in Tommy's body and decided to put a hold on the order?

I try not to watch as Frank turns on the charm, wrapping his arm around Stacy and cuddling her on the couch. The entire time, I'm sickened that she's allowing him to work his way into her heart. But maybe she's putting on a show or making the best of a bad situation. She's so used to pretending and capitulating to his demands. Maybe she's forgotten how to be genuinely happy.

He nuzzles her neck, whispers something.

It's all I can do not to go to the kitchen, get a knife, and slit his throat myself. I smile at the fantasy. I don't think I can kill him in cold blood. If he tried to hurt Tommy or Stacy, I'd do whatever it takes to protect them, but I'm not an assassin.

Or am I?

I can tell he'd like me to leave the room, but I'll be damned if I'll give him the satisfaction.

Frank looks at me a few times, raises his eyebrows, suggesting I go. I pretend not to see him and stare at the TV.

After a few minutes, I hear rustling on the couch, then they both get up.

Mom leans over and gives me a kiss on the forehead, "Goodnight, honey."

"Goodnight," I say, hugging her, realizing that tomorrow I'll probably wake up in a different body, so for me this is goodbye.

I don't want to let her go.

But Frank says, "Come on," and pulls her away, off to their bedroom where he's going to defile her.

I stare at the television, not sure what to do. Maybe I'll hit the Internet — Stacy's laptop is on the dining room table. Then I hear them laughing in their room, and what sounds like Stacy moaning.

I can't listen.

I get up, go to the front door, and close it softly behind me.

A cold breeze blows the trees in my yard, and I look up the block at the other houses, wondering if the assassin is in any of them. It's dark, and the street is quiet. There are lights behind most of the windows, but the shades are all drawn. No sign of a killer lurking in shadows.

Of course, if the assassin is well trained, I probably wouldn't see him or her. So just in case he or she is watching, I decide to wave my hands back and forth as a signal.

Come and get him. Just leave the mom and kid alone!

I wait for several minutes, but the street is dead quiet. It figures, the one time I want the assassin to kill Frank, he or she is nowhere to be found.

I head back inside and am about to lock the front door, but then decide to leave it unlocked. Maybe the assassin will sneak in in the middle of the night while I'm sleeping and on my way to tomorrow's host.

Chapter Four

I wake up to a loud purring right next to my ear.

Then a light tap-tap-tap on my face.

I open my eyes. An orange tabby, Charlie, is staring down at me with big golden eyes, waiting for breakfast. I scratch him between the ears, and he presses against my hand.

Tired, I look past him and at the clock: 6:31 a.m.

My name is Ruby Simmons, a retired schoolteacher, an amateur painter, and owner of four cats, which might be two shy of being known as "the cat lady." My body is old, and I can feel it, especially after being in such a young body yesterday. I sit up in bed and see three other cats waiting for breakfast. Two in a cat bed on the floor, one sitting on the windowsill. They begin meowing.

Another detail fills itself in. I live on Baker Street.

I'm back. But for the first time, I'm relieved. I want to know what happens to Frank, Tommy, and Stacy. But whether I can do anything to help them in this old body, I don't know.

I pull myself out of bed, body creaking and aching as I

step past the cats, all running up to me, competing to rub against my legs.

"I'll feed you; gimme a second," I say, brushing by them on my way to the bedroom window. I pull the sheer white curtains aside and peer out at the Miller house at the end of the block. Everything looks the same as I last saw it. Both cars in the driveway, no police tape on the doors. I'm not sure if I'm relieved or disappointed that the assassin didn't strike.

Followed by the cats, I head to the bathroom, splash some water on my face, then look at my reflection. Ruby is a tall black woman in her sixties with a short haircut, hair mostly still dark. She looks a lot younger than her body feels to me. Prompted by a memory of her morning routine, I return to my nightstand and open the drawer for my morning meds.

I'm surprised to see a pistol sitting on the nightstand and flashback to Ruby receiving the gun from her husband Keith when he first got sick. While he hadn't told her how bad the cancer was at the time, giving her a gun and the words, "I want you to be safe if I'm not around to protect you" said it all.

Fortunately, she's not had occasion to use the gun — yet.

I take my meds then head to the kitchen so I can take care of the meowing, purring fuzzballs.

Once I put down their food, the cats completely forget me and get to the business of devouring their breakfast. One of them, a fat black-and-white female named Oreo, is particularly noisy, purring loud enough to sound like she has a broken motor.

I leave the cats to their food, get dressed, then head out the front door. Ruby takes a walk every morning and evening, so this gives me an excuse to walk by Frank's house.

I push past the white picket gate at the end of my sidewalk, look to my left, and see Old Man Wilbur sitting on his porch swing, pretending to read the paper.

He sees me and raises his hand in a wave. "Good morning, Ruby!"

"Morning, Wilbur." My best attempt at a smile is kind but does nothing to invite conversation. Ruby has endured too many chats with Wilbur, particularly since his wife passed away a year ago. Though she feels sorry for him, she doesn't like him and is pretty sure he's called code enforcement on her a few times. He calls for petty things, like not taking her trash can in on pickup day, or for letting her grass grow too tall when she's not feeling up to mowing it herself. She thinks he keeps a notebook under his paper where he writes down every perceived violation before calling them in to the city. Nothing worse than a gossiping busybody, in Ruby's opinion.

It's still a few minutes prior to Tommy's usual departure time, so I turn right, up the street rather than heading down to the end of the cul-de-sac. I try to time my walk by their house as close to their leaving as possible, and maybe overhear something to indicate how they're doing today.

As I walk up the street, Ruby's memories fill me in on each of the neighbors. She's lived here longer than nearly everyone other than Wilbur, so she knows the surrounding blocks and is friendly with most of her neighbors, even if her closest real friend, Dee, lives a half mile away. Wilbur is the only person she specifically tries to avoid.

Katherine, a single mom with twin three-year-olds, is putting her kids in the car, getting ready for daycare before heading to work.

"Hi, Kat," I call out.

"Hey, Ruby. How's it going?" she asks, straightening the car seat and strapping in one of the girls.

"Can't complain. And no point if I could, because ain't nobody listening," I comment with a laugh — I've heard a lot of old people say this, so I figure I'll try it with Ruby.

I walk up to her, peek in at the girls, and comment on how cute they are this morning.

"How are you?" I ask Kat.

"I'll let you know after I get some Starbucks. The girls decided that today would be a great day to wake up at 4:30."

"Oh, my," I say, looking at them.

They giggle at me, clueless that waking their mom so early is not a good thing.

"Yeah, it's gonna be one of those kinds of days," Kat says. "See ya later."

"Have a good one."

I continue on my walk then pick up my pace when I feel like it's nearly time for Stacy and Tommy to leave.

I hear a slamming door and turn to my right, the house next to Frank's, and see Craig Carson, a math teacher at Tommy's school, storm out of his house looking pissed. He's usually a jovial guy, especially when he's hosting a block party with his next-door neighbor, Ruben Santiago. It's surprising to see him so angry.

Then I get a flash of his wife, Colleen, who has always seemed a bit standoffish — cold whenever Ruby's been around her. Maybe they had a fight.

Craig, not seeing me, gets in his car, slams the door, backs out, then screeches away.

I look over and see that Wilbur is sitting up, alert like a prairie dog, watching everything.

I roll my eyes and keep walking.

Right in front of Frank's house, I kneel down and re-tie

the laces on my tennis shoes, stalling for time.

The front door opens, and Stacy and Tommy come outside.

I stand back up, wipe the dirt from my jeans, and offer my widest smile. "Good morning!"

"Good morning," Stacy says, smiling, her spirits looking good.

Tommy, on the other hand, looks either tired or sad. He gives a sullen wave and climbs into the passenger's side of Stacy's car.

She looks at me, embarrassed. "I'm sorry. He's in one of those moods."

"Is Tommy okay?" I ask.

"Yeah, just the usual moody preteen stuff."

"From Tommy? He's always so nice."

"Yes, but he's still twelve."

I nod. "Ah, yes, I remember."

Flashes of Ruby's own kids, she has three, now all grown and with families of their own, run through my head. They seem like good kids, but there were battles in the house growing up.

"Have a good day, Mrs. Simmons."

"You too," I say.

I notice Frank standing in the living room window, watching.

I wave at him, wanting to acknowledge that I see him and won't be cowed into pretending otherwise.

He lets the curtain fall closed.

Maybe today will be the day he gets his, I hope, walking back toward my house.

As I'm nearing Wilbur's place, he's up and off his porch, lingering near the end of the sidewalk waiting to intercept me. Ruby hates gossips, and I can feel her distaste in my mouth as I draw closer.

"Hey, Ruby, how's it going?" He steps into the street, newspaper folded under his arm.

He's shorter than Ruby by a few inches. Even though they might be around the same age, mid-sixties, he's out of shape, sickly, and looks to be at least ten years her senior. He also has beady eyes, which make me feel dirty when they're on me.

"Wow, that was something, eh?" he says, probably referring to Craig storming out of the house.

"What's that?" I ask, playing dumb.

"Craig and Colleen," he says in a conspiratorial whisper, "though can't say I'm surprised, what with the way he's been sniffin' around Stacy."

I want nothing to do with this gossip, but I'm too curious not to find out what he's talking about.

"Stacy? What do you mean?"

He looks back and forth then draws closer, still whispering, "Oh, you don't know?"

"Know what?" I ask, losing patience as he is obviously deriving a lot of pleasure from airing the neighborhood's dirty laundry.

"Well, just between you and me," he says, with a sinister grin, "I think they're sneaking around."

"*Sneaking around?* Stacy and Craig?"

He nods.

"As in sleeping together?"

He nods again then shakes his head like he's disappointed in them, and not reveling in their supposed sinful relationship. "Such a shame."

"I don't know," I say, "I can't imagine that."

"Oh, you don't see the things I see. I've seen them going to one another's houses quite a few times when Frank and Colleen are at work."

"So, they're neighbors, that doesn't mean they're

cheating."

Wilbur looks at me, nose twisted, probably repulsed that I'm not buying into his salacious rumor mongering.

"I hope you wouldn't think *I'm* cheating when I go to visit any of the gentlemen on this block. Who knows, maybe someone is watching us right now and thinking *we're cheating.*"

I wink, but he doesn't laugh. Maybe he realizes I'm making fun of him, though he doesn't seem that perceptive when the joke's on him.

"No, people wouldn't think that of you. You're not a whore."

I'm barely able to hide my shock at the word. *Whore?* Where is he getting this from?

"Whore?"

"I've said too much."

It's obvious he wants me to ask for more, but I'm disgusted and don't want to offer the pleasure.

"Never mind," I say, and start to walk away.

He calls out, "She slept around … a lot."

He got my attention. I turn back around. "Stacy?"

"Yeah, a lot."

"Where did you hear that?"

"Frank told me one night when he was drunk. Said that after she lost her first husband, who died in prison," he whispers, "that she *really* got around. Slept with more than fifteen people, he says."

"No way," I say. "Not Stacy."

Wilbur nods, "Oh, yes, Stacy."

"Did you ever consider the source?"

"Frank?"

"Yeah, he was drunk, probably in another one of his moods, and decided to spread a vicious rumor."

"I dunno. Seemed pretty convincing to me. Besides,

why would a man ever tell another man that his woman is a whore unless it's true? No man wants to be known for settling down with a tramp."

I really, *really* want to hurt this troglodyte. But I bite my tongue, so as not to do anything that might come back to bite Ruby in the ass once I'm gone. Sure, Wilbur is all buddy-buddy-nice with me now, but I know that if he had some dirt on me, the jerk would be sidling up to another of the neighbors, trashing me just the same. He's a sad little man, and the world won't miss him when he's dead.

I decide to defend Stacy, even though it's a lost cause with such a small-minded man. "First, I'm not sure I trust Frank's power of recall when he's wasted. I've heard him say some outlandish stuff. Second, whatever she did after her husband died, who are we to judge? It had to be tough on her, especially being a single mother and all."

His eyes look to the ground, and he lets out a "Maybe." I'm not sure if I got through to him or if he's trying to avoid an argument. Guys like this aren't the quarreling kind. They're spineless when it comes to face-to-face alter- cations, preferring to sow seeds of dissent in the darkness like the spiteful cowards they are.

I throw him a rope to avoid burning bridges. "Besides, I'm sure you were quite the ladies' man when you were younger, right? That didn't make *you* a whore."

He laughs, purses his lips like he's about to say some- thing, but then thinks better of it. "All right, well, I better get back inside. Got a doctor's appointment to get ready for."

I feign to care. "Oh, is everything okay?"

"Yeah, yeah, just a routine checkup, knock on wood."

I make a knocking motion, smile, and say, "Good luck, Wilbur."

I head back to the house, unable to think about

anything but this new information. Did Stacy really sleep with a bunch of men after her husband died? If so, is this something that Frank is still seething about? Something that will present a danger to her and Tommy? I can't imagine that it's true — I didn't get that vibe from Stacy, nor did I have any flashes about that while in Frank. But maybe she was on a self-destructive bender, fueled by sadness and anger over her husband dying in jail. Maybe fueled by guilt?

But why would Stacy be feeling guilty?

I'd like to write off her history as behind her, but the past has a way of stretching into the present. Maybe sleeping with Craig is another self-destructive path.

Frank being home alone with nothing but time to stew in his anger and grow more suspicious, maybe dig up some evidence of Stacy's infidelity — it's a recipe for disaster.

Before heading back into Ruby's house, I look around for any sign of the assassin.

But the street is still empty.

I SPEND much of my morning trying to preoccupy myself with busy work around Ruby's house, specifically outside, in hopes of seeing the assassin. I do some weeding in the yard, water her garden, and talk to a few neighborhood joggers as they're passing, including a woman pushing an adorable baby in a jogging stroller.

After lunch, and sitting for a bit, it hurts to stand. Maybe I pushed this old body too hard. I hope Ruby doesn't pay the price tomorrow for my activities today.

"Sorry, Ruby," I say looking at my reflection in the kitchen window.

I spend some time petting the cats, giving them treats

while stopping by the window every now and again to look outside at Frank's.

His car hasn't budged.

If he had plans to look for a job, he must be doing it online.

Yeah, right. He's more likely getting drunk.

Soon enough, I realize it's almost time for Tommy's bus to arrive. I decide to take another walk, maybe swing by his stop to make sure Evan and the bullies don't get off with Tommy to make good on Evan's threat.

I round the block and see the bus coming. There are about fifteen houses along the right side of the road before Tommy's stop.

I pick up my pace but am instantly punished with pain in my feet. I slow my gait but am still probably walking faster than Ruby typically does.

The bus stops, and kids pour out. A lot more kids than normally get off at Tommy's stop.

I'm still six houses away.

I see Tommy disembark, with Evan and his goons right behind him.

Kids are crowding around, waiting for the inevitable fight.

The bus doors close, and the bus pulls away.

Why is the bus driver leaving? Can't she see a kid is about to get his ass kicked?

Three houses away.

I walk faster.

Tommy is approaching, though I'm not sure if he sees me, or would even recognize his neighbor when all he probably wants to do is get home.

"Hey, faggot!" Evan yells then runs up behind Tommy and punches him right in the back of the head.

Two houses away.

Evan and three of his friends circle Tommy on the ground. Other kids crowd around them, and I lose sight of Tommy.

My heart is racing with the loud chanting: *Fight, fight, fight!*

One house away.

Tommy cries out. Someone hit or kicked him.

I'm pushing my way through the crowd. Kids eye me like I'm crazy. I don't care.

"Get the hell out of my way!" I yell at the kids still blocking my path.

They turn, startled, and part.

Now it's just Evan and two of his goons surrounding Tommy.

Evan is kicking Tommy in the ribs and back, eyes wild, his face redder than his hair.

"Hey!" I run up and shove him.

Evan takes a step back, eyes wide, surprised, "Who the fuck are you?"

His friends look too shocked to say a word.

"I'm the bitch that's gonna kick your ass if you don't back the fuck off!"

Wide eyes from Evan and friends.

Laughter from the kids around me.

I turn and glare at them, let them know I mean business.

Evan steps toward me, and I wonder if he'd really hit an old lady.

Is he that crazy?

I meet his gaze.

Even though I'm sure he could do some real harm, and it's not my body I'm risking, I stand my ground, refusing to let this punk-ass kid scare me. While Ruby's body is old and achy, she's not frail. She gets regular exercise. And

Vinnie's fighting instincts are still coursing through my mind. I can feel it like a hot pan begging for butter.

"Come on," I say, raising my fists.

Evan breaks out into laughter, pointing at me, "Oh, look at this shit. This old bitch thinks she can take me!"

He's laughing, but there's no mistaking the fear in Evan's eyes. Or his friends'. Yeah, he'd probably win in a fight, but how many good licks would I get in? How embarrassed would he be?

Evan and his friends are slowly backing away. "Some pussy you are, Tommy," Evan says. "Having your grandma come and fight your battles for you."

"Grandma that's gonna kick your ass if you don't get to steppin'," I say, pulling out a phrase Ruby's husband had once yelled at a couple of thugs trying to mug them one night while they were walking home from the movies. Keith was a big, intimidating man, so the phrase was a bit more menacing from the mouth of someone his size. Still, it felt good to use one of Ruby's memories against these punks.

Evan says, "Fuck this shit. You go ahead and run home with grandma, *Tammy*. We'll finish this another time."

"The hell you will," I say. "You mess with Tommy again, I'll find you."

I want to add something more threatening, but don't want to get Ruby in trouble with the police, or put her on Evan and his thugs' radar, if they were bold enough to start messing with her. I have to remember that while I have the skills to defend her now, her experience is different without me in her body.

Evan turns around and leaves with his friends.

The remaining kids disperse.

Tommy looks up at me, eyes wide, bloodied lip trembling, "Th-thank you, Mrs. Simmons."

In addition to his bloody lip, Tommy has fresh bruises on his left cheek, and probably welts along his back and ribs. Hell, he's lucky if his ribs aren't broken, the way Evan was going to town.

He must see my concern because now he's on the verge of tears and looking himself up and down. "I can't go home like this."

"Why not?"

"Frank will be piss ... mad if he knows I got beat up. He's been trying to teach me to fight for the past year, and—"

Tommy breaks off into a coughing fit then winces, gingerly touching his right rib cage.

"Here," I say, offering my hand to help him up, "come to my house, and I'll fix you up."

I'm not sure if I can get rid of the evidence. His lips and bruised face will look worse before they look better. But maybe I can calm his nerves and figure out what to tell Frank, or maybe call his mom to come home early and serve as a buffer.

He takes my hand.

The slightest spark of static electricity shocks us both.

We laugh, but as we start to walk back to my house, I wonder if that shock is indicative of something else.

I'd had a similar sensation when touching people who were housing another Jumper. But judging from Tommy's response, and the lack of any weird momentary light in his eyes, I don't think there's a Jumper inside him.

So, what was the shock? Is it something I get when making physical contact with a body I've been in before? Or something more ominous?

~

Tommy is sitting in Ruby's living room, giving three of the cats — the fourth is off hiding — all the attention they can take.

I let him use Ruby's bathroom to take a shower, while I scrub some of the grime from his pants and shirt. I can't get all the stains out, at least not without doing a load of laundry, which we don't have time for, but I clean the clothes as much as I can. Once dressed, I tend to a few of Tommy's wounds, just to make sure nothing was broken, and give him some bandages. He'll probably be in a lot of pain tomorrow.

Despite my best efforts to get him fixed up, I don't think he'll be able to hide the fight.

I bring a pitcher of tea into the living room, set it on the glass coffee table in between my chair and his couch, then return with two glasses and pour us each a drink.

"Thank you," he says, sipping.

"You're welcome. I was going to bring lemonade, but then figured it might sting your lip. I hope you like tea. Let me know if it's sweet enough."

"It's good," he says, wiping his mouth with the back of his hand and putting the makeshift cold pack — a bag of ice wrapped in paper towels — back to his lip.

I take a drink of tea. It's good, though maybe not as sweet as I generally drink it.

While two of the cats continue to walk back and forth rubbing against Tommy's pants, Oreo has hopped up onto the couch to snuggle beside him.

"Ah, she likes you."

He smiles. "We used to have a cat named Snickerdoodle, but she ran away a week after we moved in with Frank."

"I'm sorry to hear that. You all didn't get another cat?"

"No, Frank doesn't seem to like them very much."

When Tommy says that, I get a picture of Frank secretly taking the cat into the woods and letting it go. Or hell, maybe killing it. It's not one of his memories, I don't think, but I wouldn't put anything past him.

Asshole.

"Well, you can come here and visit my cats and me anytime."

"Thanks."

"I get the feeling he doesn't like very many things," I say, moving the conversation to Frank.

Tommy looks up at me, and I'm worried that I crossed the line.

"What do you mean?"

"I don't know, just a vibe I get from him. Not like your mom, she's the sweetest person on the block. But Frank? Not so much."

Tommy laughs. "Yeah, he's a dick."

His blunt word choice makes me choke on my tea. He looks up at me, eyes nervous like he might have offended me. I can't help but laugh.

Soon, we're both laughing.

"Sorry. Just figured with the way you were talking to Evan and them at the bus stop, you were a lot cooler than a lot of old, er, *older* people."

The way he fumbles over his words is charming, though I feel bad knowing how he also suffers from a constant fear of saying something that might upset Frank.

"It's okay; I am old. And you're 100 percent correct. Frank *is* a dick."

Tommy laughs again.

"So, you said he tried teaching you to fight?"

"Yeah, I got into it with some kid last year, and he destroyed me. Frank was mad. At first, it felt good that he was so upset that someone had hurt me. It meant that he *did* care about me. He offered to teach me to fight, three times a week in the garage. But then I realized he was only doing it to torment me. He'd call me names: *wimp, faggot, wussy*, all the things other kids were already calling me. He said he was doing it to toughen me up, but I dunno, seemed like he enjoyed it as much as the bullies."

"So, what happened? Did he teach you to fight?"

"No, mostly he just knocked me down. To be fair, he did try to teach me some moves, but I'm not very coordinated, and I couldn't really counter his blows. I always wound up on the ground. So finally, I just said thank you, but no thank you."

"And how did he take that?"

"Not well. He threw a fit, complained to my mom that I needed to man up or I was never gonna get anywhere in life. I don't know what she said to get him off my case, but he eventually stopped trying to teach me. But I know when I go home, it's gonna be one big *See, I told ya* … I *hate* when he's right."

"I'm sure everything will be all right." I'm not sure why I said that, especially with Frank being such a volatile man.

Tommy takes a long sip of tea, sets his glass down, and meets my eyes. "Everything won't be fine."

"What do you mean?"

I wonder if he's going to tell me about Stacy's confession, that Frank threatened to kill them if they ever left. And what will I do with that information if he does? What advice do I give him? And what will that mean for Tommy and Ruby's friendship tomorrow or the next day when I'm in another body? Will she remember what he told her? Will she act on it in a way that puts Tommy, Stacy, and maybe even herself in more danger?

I don't like where this conversation is headed, but what

can I do — tell Tommy to shut up and go home? No, I need to be here for him, whatever he decides to say to me.

"Frank is a bad person," he says, measuring his words.

I decide to nod, let him get out whatever he wants to say.

"He hits my mom. He hit me a couple of nights ago."

"He *hits* you all?" I say, acting surprised.

"Yeah. It's not as bad as … well, what Evan was doing to me. Just a slap here and there when he explodes. But that's not the worst of it."

Oh boy, here we go.

I wait.

He continues, eyes tearing up. "No, the worst is the things he says to her. He's always calling her things like stupid, bitch, whore, and just always putting her down."

He shakes, about to burst into tears. "She's not any of those things, though. She's my mom. She's awesome. She works hard, she's smart, she's funny, and she's way cooler than any other mom I know. She's my best friend."

Tommy breaks down.

I move to the couch and put my arms around him. He leans against me, crying against my shoulder.

I want to wrap him up and protect him from that monster, keep him and his mother safe.

But what can I do? I won't be here tomorrow. Even if I am, I'm making choices with Ruby's body. If I confront Frank, hell, even if I went and did the absolute worst, and murdered him, I'm committing another person to *my* decision. Someone else would suffer my consequences. Someone else would go to jail, or maybe wind up in the crossfire as Frank's victim.

I feel as helpless as Tommy.

I hug him harder.

After a minute, he pulls away, maybe embarrassed by

the outpour of emotion, and looks down at the ground.

I want to say something to help him. But what? Do I tell him to go to the police? We all know how that usually turns out. The police can't provide constant protection for Tommy and his mother, or be there to stop Frank when he finally explodes. They can only enforce a court order, or respond to a crime scene after the fact.

I'd love to go over to Frank's right now and put a bullet through his head. I wish I'd not intervened when the assassin was about to do it a few days ago.

God, if I knew then what I know now.

Tommy stands. "I should go. I'm sure Frank's probably looking for me by now."

He gives Oreo one last scratch between her ears. The cats at his feet look disappointed by his obvious departure.

I'm still struggling to find the right thing to say.

"Tommy, if you need me, if you need anything, please don't hesitate to come over or call me. Do you have my number?"

"No, I don't think we do."

I go to the kitchen, find a piece of paper, and scratch Ruby's number down as it comes to me. I hand him the paper. "I'm serious, Tommy. Anything. You all don't have to go through this alone."

"Thank you," he says, meeting my eyes. He puts the ice pack to his lip, then pulls it away. "Mrs. Simmons?"

"Yes?"

"Do you think it's ever right to do the wrong thing for the right reason?"

"What do you mean?"

He pauses, as if trying to articulate his thoughts, then shakes his head, "Never mind."

He opens the door, steps outside onto the porch.

"Wait," I say, "what do you mean?"

Tommy looks toward his house, sees Frank standing outside looking up the street. "Oh, crap, there he is. I've gotta go. Thanks again, Mrs. Simmons."

Tommy jogs off my step and heads home.

I close the door, head back to my bedroom, and peer through the curtains, watching Frank meet the boy.

He turns Tommy's face, examining the wound, asks him something I can't hear, probably along the lines of "What the hell happened?"

Rather than embrace Tommy or offer him any form of comfort, Frank makes a disgusted face then turns and stomps into the house.

Tommy follows.

I find myself wondering what Tommy meant by his question: *Is it ever right to do the wrong thing for the right reason?*

I hope he's not about to do anything stupid.

I spend the rest of the night wondering what Tommy meant, and what he might be planning to do. I don't remember seeing any alarming memories while I was in him. Maybe this is something new.

I wonder if I should call Stacy and warn her that Tommy might be about to do something stupid, but what could she do? If anything, Stacy might escalate the problem.

What is the assassin waiting for?

I'M in Frank's house.

I know this can't possibly be real, so it must be a dream. But here's the thing — I haven't dreamed in a year. I don't know where *I* go when the host's body sleeps, but I don't think I'm in them once I lose consciousness. I'm not even sure if I ever sleep.

But now I am in a dream in Tommy's bedroom. I'm in his bed, staring out his window as rain pelts it with a million liquid nails. Lightning flashes, thunder exploding loud enough to shake the walls. I feel it in my bones.

I draw the sheets tighter, pulling them over my body, afraid.

Suddenly, Tommy's door violently shakes — someone trying to get in. Is it Frank? It must be. But why isn't he saying anything, demanding that Tommy opens the door? It isn't like Frank to keep his big mouth shut.

The door shakes louder, so hard, I'm sure it will fly off its hinges.

I climb out of bed, looking for a weapon, something to defend myself. I find a bat in the closet, then stop in front of the mirror and am surprised to see that I'm not in Tommy's body.

I have no body at all.

The bat floats in the mirror as if held by a ghost.

The door continues to shake.

Suddenly, I hear Stacy crying, "No, don't!"

The door stops shaking.

There's screaming from the other side, Frank shouting incoherently.

A gunshot explodes.

Silence.

I stare at the door.

Oh, God, Frank did it. He shot Stacy.

No, no, no.

I can't move.

Footsteps approaching. He's coming for me, or maybe Tommy.

A knock on the door.

No, go away, I'm not answering.

Another knock …

Chapter Five

I WAKE to three loud knocks.

I turn and see a bright, blinding light on my face.

I jump, startled, then realize I've woken in a car. The light to my left is from the officer who knocked on my window.

Now that the cop has my attention, he makes a circular motion with his left hand meaning he wants me to roll down the window. His right hand is on his gun, still holstered in his belt. He's tall, broad-shouldered, in his late thirties, with thick dark hair hinting at gray on the sides. His expression is all business.

I fumble in the unfamiliar car for the button, hit it, but nothing happens.

Then I remember to turn on the car. I look for keys, then remember the start button. I push it and roll down the window, knowing the cop is likely taking my confusion for inebriation.

"You okay, sir?"

I see the clock. It reads, *5:15 a.m.* Not a good hour to be found sleeping in the car.

"Yeah," I say, though my back and head are both throbbing. From the corner of my eye, I see a second officer at the passenger side door, flashing a light through the cabin.

"Do you mind explaining why you're here?" the cop asks.

I realize I'm in the parking lot of Tommy's middle school.

Why am I here?

I'm still waiting for information on my host's details, like a name, or something. Anything. I certainly don't know why I'm sleeping in a school parking lot.

Am I a teacher?

Yes, that's it. I *am* a teacher.

Not just a teacher, but Craig Carson, the neighbor that Old Man Wilbur thinks is screwing around with Stacy. The man I watched storm out of his house.

"I work here," I mumble, trying not to sound drunk. I'm not sure if Craig did get drunk last night. I don't see any alcohol lying around, but I sure feel hungover.

"And what, you live in the parking lot?"

"My wife kicked me out last night," I say, details coming as they fall from my mouth. "I was driving around all night trying to figure out how to make things right, then decided not to bother with a hotel when I've gotta be at work early. Figured I'd come here, then shower and change in the gym before school started."

"License and registration, please," the cop says. "And do you have a school ID?"

"Yes, sir." I fumble through the glove box, then my wallet, to get him everything he needs.

Both cops retreat to their patrol car where they're probably running my plate and checking my story. I realize how damn cold it is in the car, then roll up my window and turn on the heat.

My heart is racing. I feel moments from puke.

I have vague flashes of an argument Craig had with his wife, Colleen, but can't remember the details. Did she discover the affair?

Was he even having an affair with Stacy?

If so, I don't remember one. I wish I had more control over my hosts' memories, or that I could direct them and get information. How can I take control of their bodies and feel so many of their emotions yet not tap into their brains to get everything I need? If this is a system put in place by whoever put assassins in the field, their engineers, scientists, or whatever, got it way wrong.

Maybe it's not an exact science.

Another knock at my window yanks me from my thoughts.

The officer is back, my license, ID, and proof of insurance in his hands, though he's not yet handing them back.

"If we did a breathalyzer now, would you blow positive?"

"I haven't been drinking, sir. Just a rough night, I swear."

He stares into my eyes, and I'm nervous not knowing what he'll see. Maybe he'll sense something is wrong, even if he isn't sure what, then pull me out and arrest me.

I remember my dream.

I don't know what it meant. Only that I need to find Stacy and Tommy to make sure they're okay. Maybe in Craig's body I can convince them to leave Frank once and for all. I don't have a plan after that, but we'll figure something out.

But first I need to get these cops to leave. If they think I'm drunk and arrest me, my day is shot.

I maintain eye contact with the officer, just enough to show I'm not hiding anything, but not enough to make him think I'm psychotic or on drugs.

His expression goes from suspicious to understanding. Maybe he can relate to Craig's problems, or feels a kinship in that we both have demanding, thankless jobs. I'm not sure what it is, but he's moved enough to hand me my license, work ID, and proof of insurance.

"Okay, sir, I suggest you find somewhere else to sleep tomorrow night."

"Thank you, officer."

He heads back to his car. A few minutes later, the cruiser leaves, and I'm left alone in the dark lot. I can't stop thinking about the dream. The only one I've had since I started Jumping. It wasn't just terrifying, the dream was ominous, maybe prophetic.

It sounds silly to think I somehow glimpsed the future, but considering everything else that's happened to me, prophetic dreams aren't even especially crazy.

But how can I see the future? Is this time travel — am I getting hints of what might happen, and their prevention is up to me?

I don't know, and the lack of answers is maddening. But I do know one thing: ignoring the dream would condemn Stacy and Tommy to tragedy.

I have to do something.

I *think* I have an idea.

I pull out of the parking lot and head to Baker Street.

~

I FIND A SPOT A BLOCK AWAY, parking in front of a vacant lot and sit listening to the radio while I wait.

I'm overcome with a deluge of memories from Craig's argument with his wife.

It began rather innocuously with Colleen complaining about him working late. She asked why he never made time for her.

He said that he can't help it if he has to stay late sometimes. He's a teacher and subject to external forces — last-minute staff meetings, parent conferences, needing help from the guidance counselors after hours for problem students, and kids who ask to see him after school.

"I wish you cared as much about our marriage as your stupid job," she said. "And why *do you* put so much time for such low pay? Do you *like* being treated like shit?"

This was easy for her to say, of course, since she worked part-time for her father's air conditioning company, where she'd been since college. She'd never had a real job, one she had to earn on her merits, without carte blanche to come and go as she pleased. Colleen was also paid at least three times what her position was worth, simply because she was Daddy's Girl. She worked a third of Craig's hours but often brought home more than him, which justified her questioning his job.

To make matters worse, he sometimes agrees. Yes, his job has long hours and is often thankless. He didn't make nearly what he was worth. Add inept board members, ignorant parents who barely care to help their own children, and yes, sometimes Craig hates his job.

But he also likes making a difference. And all the crap is worth it for those few kids each year whom he could genuinely help.

She went on about his "stupid job," and Craig found himself wondering why he'd married her. And then why he stayed with her. He hadn't loved Colleen in at least eight of the ten years they'd been married, but at the same time, he was raised to believe that you didn't break a vow. You made the most of a situation, just as his parents before him had for thirty miserable years.

Craig wasn't sure if Colleen had changed after they got married, becoming more materialistic and less caring about others, or if she'd always been that way and he'd been blinded by her better qualities. She was beautiful, confident in a way that he wasn't, funny and outgoing. She challenged him in ways he'd never been challenged. Craig liked that. But after a few years, challenges became more like character attacks. She had a complaint about nearly every aspect of his personality: Craig was too into his job, he was too obnoxious when around his male friends, he didn't care enough about having bigger and better things. He was, she often said, a perpetual college kid refusing to grow up. Forget for a moment that it was she who didn't want to have children, while he'd always wanted to settle down and raise a family.

At some point, the conversation shifted, so fast and so jarringly, that he was blindsided by her accusation.

"Are you cheating on me? Are you sleeping with another teacher? Or maybe one of those single moms you're always meeting with?"

"What?" Craig said, barely able to believe the accusation.

"Well, you don't have sex with me anymore. So, who is it?"

"Nobody!"

"Bullshit."

"I'm not sleeping with anyone! I swear."

"Then why don't you touch me?"

No answer would please her.

"Maybe you wish I was more like Stacy? Is that it?"

"What?" he asked, annoyed and ashamed by the truth. He'd come to care a lot about Stacy in the past year. He'd come to know her when he had them over to tutor Tommy in math. She was everything that Colleen wasn't — warm, a nice person, a loving mother, and someone who would do anything for her family.

Yes, he'd thought about Stacy a lot. And it was more than a crush. He wasn't sure if he'd come to love her or if he just related to her because they were in similar situations — trapped with miserable people. There'd been a few times when Stacy had met him after school, and it was just the two of them in his classroom. They'd started talking about Tommy, but recently the conversations ended with her tears on his shoulder. She'd never told Craig about the death threats, but Stacy had confessed that she was sad and sometimes scared. He'd told her to call the cops, but she always backed down, saying it wasn't that bad. Seeing her cry like that, he longed to rescue her — take her and Tommy somewhere safe, where they'd be appreciated instead of abused. Not only would Craig be saving them, but he'd also be saving himself from a life sentence with Colleen.

Despite his feelings, he'd never once flirted. The fact that Colleen had somehow figured out his feelings only angered him more. She had no right to talk about their friendship, or make accusations. Craig had been faithful and would've probably remained miserable with Colleen forever.

"That's it, isn't it?" she said to his nonresponse. "You're fucking that white trash bitch."

"She's not a white trash bitch!" Craig said, jumping to Stacy's defense fast enough to curl Colleen's lip in the way that he hated.

And even though Craig hadn't intended to say what he had, he couldn't stop himself. He'd bottled the truth, putting up with her haranguing for so long, playing a charade, and for what, that he finally exploded in a single brutal moment of truth.

"You want to know why I don't touch you? I don't touch you because I can't stand to look at you!"

She stared at him, stunned, mouth agape, tears welling up.

"What?"

Instead of taking it back, Craig continued, telling Colleen how much she had changed, and that he was tired of being made to feel that he was always wrong. Tired of having to pretend that she hadn't changed for the worse, that she'd become as cold and callous as her mother. He ended with, "No, I am not sleeping with Stacy, but I'll say this — for you to call her a white trash bitch shows what's wrong with you. And if you can't see that, then I don't know that we have any hope."

Colleen's face went stone cold, lips pursed tight. She glared at Craig, her contempt no longer hidden behind crooked smiles and rolling eyes. "Get out."

"What? Get out of my own house?"

"It's more my house than yours." She was, of course, talking about the fact that her father had helped them with a generous loan for the down payment, an advance that neither Colleen nor her father would ever let him forget.

That did it. The kid gloves were off. Craig was done pretending. Done putting up with her shit. Done being made to feel worthless because he wasn't rich or *cultured* like her stuck-up asshole father.

"You know what? Fine. It's your house. Fuck you *and* your daddy."

And Craig stormed out.

As I SIT in the car watching morning light slowly nudge the shadows, I can feel the rawness of the fight as if I'd just had it myself.

No wonder Craig was sleeping in the parking lot.

I finally get out of the car and start walking toward Baker Street, hoping I can catch Stacy before she leaves, without drawing attention from Frank.

I stop at the end of Baker and wait patiently at the corner, using the cover of a tall red fence to stay out of Old Man Wilbur's line of sight. Now that I'm in Craig and have some of his memories, my blood boils at the old man's accusations that Craig and Stacy were having an affair. Hell, I wouldn't be the least bit surprised if Wilbur accidentally let his suspicions slip while chatting with Colleen, or maybe another of the neighbors who then told her.

I can see the old man sitting on the porch, using a newspaper to hide his voyeurism. How can someone devote so much of their time to spying on his neighbors, spreading gossip, and generally making other people's lives miserable? He may not be an assassin, but his chatter can have the same effects on people's lives. Maybe if the assassin comes today, Wilbur will get caught in the crossfire.

I smile at the thought.

At the end of the block, Frank's front door opens.

I step back behind the corner, waiting a moment, then peer around the fence again. Tommy is walking up the block toward the bus stop. But he isn't alone.

Frank is with him.

What the hell? Why is Frank walking him to the bus?

Maybe he's going as Tommy's protector, to stand by and make sure that Evan and his friends don't start anything. Or maybe he's going to intervene and kick their asses himself. Frank is a hothead. But having been inside his mind, I also know there's a small part of him that probably doesn't want to see Tommy hurt. Does he like Tommy? No. Does he wish Tommy lived somewhere else? Oh yeah. But he doesn't want to see the boy physically hurt by a bunch of punk kids. So maybe Frank will stand up for the boy, even if doing so might land his ass behind bars.

Come to think of it I almost *hope* Frank goes off on Evan. Maybe seriously injures the punk. Put Evan and Frank *both* out of commission for a while.

I hide as they reach the end of the block then turn to head up 112th Terrace to the bus stop.

I make a run toward Frank's house.

I'm not even part way there when Old Man Wilbur calls out from the bench, "Hello, Mr. Carson."

I turn, wave, and am eager to move on.

But he isn't done yet.

"Going to see your lover?"

I turn, angry, wanting to kill the gossip with my fists.

He stays seated on his porch swing but lowers his paper. "Of course, you're not really Craig, are you?"

He winks. I see the briefest flash of light in his eyes and realize that he isn't Old Man Wilbur.

"You?"

"The Asian woman, and the mailman, yes. Come here, come here," he says, waving me over.

"I don't have time; I have to talk to Stacy."

"You should make time. You'll want to hear what I have to say."

I step onto the porch.

"Please, sit," he says, moving his paper aside.

I don't want to sit next to him. I don't trust this man in the least, and don't want to waste whatever window I might have with Stacy to convince her to get Tommy so we can take off together. It seems like the perfect solution. I doubt Craig could take Frank in a fight or defend himself without a weapon, but I do think he's smart enough to hide them for a while until Frank either gives up looking or drinks himself to death.

"So, where are you going?" the assassin asks.

"To convince Stacy to get the hell out of her house. Frank is dangerous. Now I see why you've been trying to —"

"Kill him," the assassin says.

"Yes."

"And yet you stopped me, twice."

"I didn't know he was a monster. And for the record, I didn't try to stop you two days ago when I was Tommy. Hell, I even left his front door unlocked for you. Where were you then, or yesterday when I was Ruby?"

"I had more pressing concerns."

"What?"

"None of your business. I don't control where I go, any more than you do. Otherwise, I wouldn't be in this body today, the least-equipped body to finish this job. Which is why we need to talk."

"Talk," I say.

"I need you to kill him."

"What? No, I'm not a killer."

"I feel that today is the last possible day to get this done. And I'm afraid this body won't work."

"So you want *me* to do it? Let's say for even a moment that *I* didn't have a problem murdering someone in cold blood. What about Craig? I commit a crime in his body, and he's the one who will pay."

"That's not our problem."

"What?"

"It's not our problem. We're given these bodies to use as needed. We can't concern ourselves with what happens once we're done."

"You can't honestly believe that."

"I have a job to do — simple as that."

I shake my head, trying to make sense of what the old man is saying. "Okay, you claim you're an assassin, but you help people, right? Even though you don't know the reason, you believe it's for the greater good or something, right?"

He nods.

"Then how can you not care about the people whose bodies you're in? What good is your mission if your choices are leaving more victims behind?"

"Hey, it's not my first choice to screw Craig over. If you can find a way to do it without the guy getting caught, then by all means, please do. But you can't let your fear of getting him in trouble prevent you from doing what must be done."

"I haven't agreed to do *anything*."

He sighs deeply, then suddenly he's waving his hand.

I look up to see Frank returning home alone. He looks at us both, waves without bothering to smile, and continues along to his house.

"You have to kill him," the assassin says. "Tonight."

I've spent the past few hours sitting inside Wilbur's house with the assassin, mostly at the dining room table, looking outside, watching Frank's house, waiting for Stacy to leave so I can run out and flag her down. I guess she's not working today, but I'm hoping she'll find a reason to leave.

The assassin is going over various methods of killing people while I wait. He says that this is a refresher course — I should know this all instinctually, even if my memories are gone. To say it feels odd to have this little old man plotting murder in such a blasé manner is an understatement. He doesn't give names of victims, but he does say he's killed people of all walks of life — politicians, clergy, businessmen, stay-at-home moms.

He's sitting across from me at the dining room table, both of us drinking a beer, when I ask, "Have you killed children?"

"Of course."

I'm surprised, outraged even.

"How can you justify killing children?"

"You act like we have a say in any of this. We get the names on The List, and we do our job. I learned long ago that it's pointless to question The List."

"You don't *have to* do your job. Can't you call an audible, decide no, you're not killing a child?"

The assassin's smile is grim enough to give me chills. "You're poking. I told you I'm not getting into this. I'm sure your mind was wiped for a good reason. I won't be the one to screw things up."

"You'll ask me to do your job, but you won't tell me what I need to know?"

"You know what you need to know: Frank has to die. Tonight. Everything else is noise."

"Come on, give me something. Where are our bodies? Who is making us do this? How long before we get our lives back? If we've been hired, how are we paid? It's not like I can access some Universal Body Jumper's bank account."

"*Body Jumpers?*"

"Yeah, that's the only thing I could think to call this. You got another name?"

"I won't tell you the official one, but I'll tell you how we refer to ourselves."

"Okay, shoot."

"Karma Police."

"*Karma Police?*"

"Yes, we serve justice to those who are ordinarily beyond it."

"So, you're an organized group of body jumping vigilantes?"

"I prefer enforcers."

"Enforcing *what?* Some shadow group's arbitrary sense of justice, or *karma?* Who are *you all* to decide who lives or dies? And how can killing a child, or ruining innocent people's lives, ever be karma?"

Wilbur looks at me. "I can't expect you to understand without context. And I can't provide context without risking your wipe. Suffice it to say the system works. Though you might not always see it immediately, we're doing great things. You can't possibly argue that killing Frank is a bad thing, can you?"

I stare at the bottle in my hand, wanting another beer, but not wanting to dull my senses in case I need to spring into action soon.

As much as I'd thought about killing Frank over the past few days and how many problems it would solve for Stacy and Tommy, whenever I start considering the realistic ramifications of *actually* murdering the man in cold blood, everything crumbles.

I try to elucidate my feelings. "It's one thing to kill someone when you're defending yourself or a loved one. I can do that. I *have* done that."

The assassin raises a finger. "Oh, you've done far more than that."

I continue, unabated. "But what I cannot do, regardless of what you say I've done in the past, is kill without provocation. It's *wrong*."

"No, what's wrong is ignoring a problem you're able to fix. To ignore a growing evil as it comes closer to delivering its threats. That is what's wrong, to merely sit by and let something terrible happen when you have the foresight and ability to stop it."

"Even if I could just do it, what about the fallout? If I get caught, Craig goes to jail. But even if I don't, what about Stacy and Tommy? What if they witness the murder? How does that affect them? They'll never be the same. I can't imagine a world where a traumatized Stacy and Tommy is a *great* thing."

"I'd wager that it's a sight better than a world with a dead Stacy or Tommy, wouldn't you?"

"Is that what you're saying — that if I don't kill Frank, they're going to die?"

"I don't know what's going to happen. I have a name and a date. Beyond that, I don't know any more than you. But if that helps you justify killing Frank in some way, then yes, you should expect that their lives will be in danger if you don't do your job."

Of course, this isn't the answer I want.

I don't know why I'm so hesitant. It's not like Frank is a good guy. Being inside him, I can appreciate some of the hell he's gone through in his life, but my sympathy ended the moment he laid a finger on Stacy. Add to that his threat against her, then she and her son are prisoners of an evil man who deserves to die.

But can I walk into his house and kill him point blank?

Can I put Craig's future in jeopardy? The assassin is coercing me to kill a man for some mysterious, unknown reason he either won't tell me or doesn't know himself. The situation reeks, and I don't like being backed into a corner, with the decision ripped from my hands.

No, I need to find another way.

Suddenly, I see an opportunity.

Frank is walking to his car, wearing dress pants, a dress shirt, and a handsome red tie. He's also clean-shaven. Going on a job interview, I'm guessing. He gets into his car but isn't leaving yet.

Come on, come on.

I watch the front door, hoping and praying it won't open again only to have Stacy walk out and join him.

Come on; leave!

He pulls out of the driveway.

Yes!

I wait long enough to make sure he hasn't forgotten anything.

After a few minutes without his return, I leave Wilbur's place saying, "Maybe there's another way."

I don't wait for a response.

I KNOCK on Frank's door, heart racing.

Come on, Stacy. Open up.

No answer.

Has she already left? Maybe her car isn't working, and she got a ride to work earlier before I was waiting.

I knock again, dread in my gut that I've somehow missed her. Maybe there isn't another way. Maybe the assassin is right.

The door opens.

Stacy is standing in sweat pants and a long T-shirt. Her nose and eyes are red.

"Hey, Craig, why aren't you at school?"

"I called in sick. You sick, too?"

She nods. "Yeah, woke up feeling like crap."

She's staring at me, clearly wondering why I'm here.

"Can I come in for a second? We need to talk."

Her eyes widen. "Of course," she says, ushering me in.

My heart is a jackhammer as I try to figure out how to start. I know she and Craig have talked about Frank a number of times, and I know she cares about Craig. But I don't know if she feels the same as he does, that she'd be willing to run off with a man — a married man, no less.

Now that I'm here in front of her, my brilliant plan to save her and Tommy feels like the Dumbest Idea Ever.

"What's wrong?"

Now or never.

"I want you to run away with me."

"What?" Her face is blank. I can't tell if she's stunned or awaiting a punchline.

"I know this is going to seem crazy and out of the blue, but I love you, Stacy. I want you and Tommy to come away with me, today."

"Love? You're married. I'm … with Frank."

"I don't love my wife. She's a cold, callous person driven only by money. I thought we could make it work, but I was fooling myself. I see how kind you are, how much you care about Tommy, and how Frank treats you both. It isn't safe here, for either of you. Please, let me take you away. We can pack some bags, go get Tommy from school, and leave."

She's shaking her head.

I'm overwhelming her, I know. This is coming from nowhere. I'm asking Stacy to uproot her life and flee with me. Suddenly, I feel like maybe I've overestimated her feelings for Craig. Maybe his attraction was a one-way street. Maybe she'd never thought of him as anything but her son's math teacher, and a nice, safe married neighbor.

"I'm flattered," she says, eyes watering, "but … "

Oh no, here it comes. She doesn't feel the same. I've misread the situation, and now I have no plan to fall back on.

I double down. Move closer, grab her hands and meet her eyes.

"Tell me you don't think about me, wonder what it would be like for us to be together. Tell me you don't think about running away every night when you lie down with that monster."

Tears stream down her cheeks.

I can see it in her eyes. She *has* thought of Craig like this. The feeling *is* mutual. But her practical side won't allow the impulsivity. She's scared. Too many variables.

"I love you," I say, going all in.

She's shaking her head. "Where would we go? Frank will find us and kill us all."

"I won't let him."

She shakes her head again, smiling at me sweetly, but also like I just don't understand the danger.

"He will find us. He's told me so. If I ever leave, he'll kill Tommy and me."

"I won't let him."

"Where would we go? What would we do for money?"

"I don't know, we'll figure it out."

"I'm sorry, Craig, that's not enough. I need a plan. I need to know how we'll survive. Otherwise, I'm only moving Tommy from one scary situation to another. At least now I know we're relatively safe."

"He hits you, both of you."

"Tommy told you?"

I lie and say yes.

"Frank didn't mean to. He even offered to get counseling."

I'm not sure if she's lying or if it's something he truly agreed to, but it's no guarantee that she's safe. But how can I convince her? What do I do, tell her I had some ominous dream? Tell her an assassin told me that they're in danger?

None of those will work.

Shit. I don't know what to say.

"I have money." I'm not sure if it's true or not, but I have to ease her into this decision. I can tell she *wants* to come but needs reassurances that they'll be safe.

She's biting her lip, moving back and forth from one foot to the other. Is it possible that I've swayed her?

I press on, "He never hit Tommy before now, right? It's probably something you told yourself he'd never do. You drew a line in the sand, telling yourself it's okay as long as he only hits you, but if he hits Tommy, then you'd leave. Am I right?"

I don't wait for her answer.

"But then he did hit Tommy. And still, you stayed. So tell me, Stacy, what's the next line in the sand? And how long before it's crossed? How many more lines will you draw before Frank finally goes too far? Before he makes good on his threat?"

She's crying, looking around the living room, maybe trying to convince herself to escape this reality, to take a chance.

"I don't know, Craig. Yes, I have feelings for you. You're great with Tommy. And I'd be lying if I said I hadn't wished you were my boyfriend instead of Frank. Wished that you weren't married. But this is a lot to ask. And Frank is trying. He really is. He's at a job interview now. I think as long as he has work that he likes, and self-confidence, he won't drink or be dangerous to Tommy and me."

"Come on, Stacy, you know there will always be some reason to justify his behavior. Some reason he reverts to what he is — a raging drunk. Stop making excuses and thinking he'll change. People like Frank only change for the worse."

"I don't know," she says.

Feeling confident that she's with me, and that I only need to get her out of the house, I say, "Pack what you need. I'm gonna get my car. It's parked on the next block. I'll be back in ten minutes. Okay?"

"I don't know."

"I'm not taking no for an answer, Stacy. You deserve to be happy, you and Tommy both."

I walk out the front door.

I hope to God that she'll be ready when I return.

I run to my car, then race back to the house, hoping Frank hasn't come home. I park on the lawn and leave the car running, no time to waste.

I run into the house, see that Stacy has four bags packed.

I smile.

Yes, we're going to do this!

I hug her. "Thank you, Stacy, you won't regret this."

She hugs me back.

A part of me wants to kiss her, but I don't want to waste another second. We need to hit Tommy's school before Frank gets home.

I grab three of the bags, and head for the door.

I step onto the lawn and open my trunk.

"Craig?"

I look up and see Colleen shouting from the street, walking toward us.

Oh, shit. Not this. Not now.

Stacy joins me at the trunk, bag in hand, whispering, "Oh, no."

"What the hell are you doing?" Colleen shouts.

"Not now," I say.

Colleen gets between me and the open driver's side door, blocking my entrance.

"So what? You two are running off together?"

"It's not like that," Stacy says, her voice cracking.

"You fucking whore!" Colleen snaps, glaring at her. Colleen breaks into a run, racing around the car, about to attack Stacy.

I yell, "Get in the car!"

She gets in then yanks the door closed and locks the door.

Colleen pounds on the passenger window. "You fucking whore!"

I'm torn. Do I try and calm Colleen, or get in the car and take off, leaving her to stew in anger?

Suddenly, a screeching of breaks.

I look up to see Frank's car slide to a halt in front of mine.

Oh, fuck.

Colleen bursts into laughter, now glaring at me. "Oh, *this* is gonna be good!"

Frank practically flies from his car, arms in the air as he gets in front of my car. "What the hell is going on here?"

He's staring right at me, ready to fight.

Colleen responds before I can speak. "He's cheating on me, with your girlfriend, and now they're gonna run off together!"

Frank's eyes are wide. He turns to Stacy, sitting in my car, terrified. "Is this true?"

She stares, unable to speak.

"Get out!" he yells at her.

"No, stay put, Stacy," I yell. "We're leaving."

"The hell you are!" Frank rushes at me.

I dodge, at the last possible second. He flies right by me and falls to the ground.

I turn, preparing for the next attack.

He comes at me again, and I go to dodge. But this time he anticipates and brings a fist hard into my chest.

I fall back against my car door, gasping for air.

My mind flashes back to when Evan knocked the wind out of Tommy, and how quickly his friends descended.

Frank grabs me by the neck, squeezing tight as he yells at Stacy. "Get the fuck out, now!"

She's crying, looking at me, terrified of what Frank is going to do. "Let him go!"

I manage to kick Frank between the legs, hard.

He lets go of me, falling back onto the driveway.

I launch myself at Frank, drop on top of his waist, straddling him.

Now it's me choking him.

He reaches up, trying to claw at my face.

"Fuck you," I yell, fingers squeezing tight as he struggles to push his neck down, trying to lessen my grip on this throat.

"Stop!" Colleen screams. "You're going to kill him."

Yes, yes I am.

I stare into Frank's eyes, bulging as his face turns bright red, spittle flying from his lips.

This isn't what I planned, but it'll do.

"I'm calling the police!" Colleen yells.

I look up at her to see her dialing.

I don't care.

I look down at Frank, dozens of shitty things he's done to Stacy and Tommy flash through my mind, fueling my bloodlust.

Now I can end it.

Now I can end him.

Another scream: "Stop!"

But it's not Colleen, it's Stacy, out of the car, rushing toward me.

She grabs me from behind by my shoulders. "Stop it; you're gonna kill him!"

Yeah, I know. Frank needs to die.

But I can't say that.

And as I hear Stacy's cry not to kill Frank, I find that I can't go through with it.

I let go, standing up and backing away, gasping as I throttle my rage.

Frank gasps, holding his throat, sucking deep breaths into his lungs.

I stare down at my shaking fists, then at Frank, now being cradled by Stacy.

What the hell?

I stare, confused. Why is she caring for him? Why did she save him? He's a monster. How many times has he hit her? He struck her son. He's probably gonna do it, or worse, again. And yet there she is by his side.

"Get out of here!" Colleen yells at me.

I stare at her now, unable to move. I don't want to leave, not without Stacy.

"I called the cops," Colleen says. As angry as she was a moment ago, this almost sounds like a warning, like she doesn't want to see me in jail.

"Go!" she yells again.

Frank glares at me. Stacy helps him stand.

I go to the trunk, grab Stacy's bags and drop them on the driveway without a word.

Then I get in the car and leave.

IT'S SEVEN AT NIGHT, and this time I've parked two blocks away.

I've been hiding for hours, afraid that the police are looking for me, scared they'll arrest me. But I wasn't about to skip town. I went and saw two movies instead. Then dinner after that.

Instead of heading down Baker, I turn in one street over, remembering that the house behind Old Man Wilbur's is a rental that's vacant. I climb the fence then knock on Wilbur's back door, hoping the assassin is still inside him, hoping he didn't take an afternoon nap and abandon his host.

After a few minutes, he answers, looking through his back window, shaking his head. He opens the door, lets me in, and says, "Why didn't you follow through? You had him."

"I don't know. Colleen was calling the cops, then Stacy was crying, begging me not to kill him. She tried pulling me off, and I just couldn't do it."

"Why?"

"I don't know! I don't know if I choked, or if I was afraid Craig would go to jail if I went through with it, or what. I think I was pretty far past self-defense, plus I *was* on his property. Craig would've been screwed."

"Pathetic." The assassin shakes his head.

"I'm sorry," I say, mad at both having to apologize and at myself for not being able to follow through, even though I hadn't intended to kill Frank in the first place.

"So, what are you going to do?"

I don't know. I say nothing.

"Obviously, you came back for a reason. I assume you're here to finish the job."

I go to the front of the house, look out at Frank's. "What happened after I left?"

"They went inside. Heard him yelling for quite a while. Heard her crying. But I don't know what else happened."

"What about Tommy?"

"He got a ride home from some kids. He seemed okay."

"Good."

"How are we going to fix this?"

"What do you want me to do? Go knock on his door and ask him to come outside so I can finish the job?"

"That would be a start."

"Yeah, like he's gonna open the door for me. If you're so keen on killing him, why don't you do it?"

"Do you have a gun? I'll do it if you've got a gun."

Then I remember — the gun in Ruby's nightstand.

"I think I can get one."

"You get it; I'll finish the job."

I wait outside on Ruby's porch as the light goes on.

She peers through the curtains hanging in the window next to her door. Her eyes widen. I'm not sure if she's scared to see me, or just surprised.

She opens the door. "Craig! Are you okay?"

"I need some help, and you're the only person I can turn to."

She lets me in, brings me to the living room where we sit beside one another on her couch. I explain as much as I can, how Stacy and Tommy are in danger. I lie, hoping she hasn't spoken to Stacy, saying that she told me how Frank is abusing them. I even suggest that Frank may be sexually abusing Tommy. That's why I was at Frank's house earlier, because Stacy asked me to take them away. Then Frank came home early, and the whole thing went to shit.

Though I hate telling such a big lie, the effect is exactly what I was aiming for. She sighs then says, "That poor boy. I knew something was going on." She wants to help. Asks what I need.

"I need a gun." Of course, I can't tell her that I know she has one. Instead, I ask if she knows where I might be able to get one. I explain that she's the only person on the block that I trust enough to ask. Everyone else is under Frank's spell.

Her lips are pursed as she considers, then asks, "What are you going to do with a gun, Craig? Are you going to shoot Frank?"

"No, I just want to help them get out."

"Why not go to the police? Have Stacy file an order of protection, tell them what Frank is doing to Tommy."

"I'm scared, Mrs. Simmons. I'm scared what'll happen if the police show up to the house. Frank won't let the cops take them. He's told Stacy that if she ever leaves, or calls the cops, he'll kill her and Tommy."

Ruby sighs, deeper this time, runs her hands through her hair, then stands from her chair.

"Hold on a second, dear."

She goes to her bedroom.

I wait, anxiously, leg bouncing uncontrollably. I'm almost there. I can get the gun, give it to the assassin, and he'll finish the job. He'll save Stacy and Tommy.

I have no idea what will happen after that. Will Wilbur get arrested for murder? Will Stacy and Tommy be traumatized? Will Stacy and Craig ever get together, or has that been ruined?

I'm scared of the possibilities, all the unknown variables, but at least Frank will be out of the picture, Stacy and Tommy will be safe, and Craig will avoid prison.

"Oh, my God," I hear Ruby say from the bedroom.

I get up to see what's wrong. She has her nightstand drawers both pulled out, along with her dresser drawers.

"What's wrong?" I ask.

"It's gone."

"What's gone?"

"My gun."

I flash back to Tommy asking Ruby "is it ever okay to do the wrong thing for the right reason?" He'd just left Ruby's bedroom after he'd showered, changed, and likely found her loaded gun.

Oh, God.

I RACE from Ruby's without explanation.

I've gotta get to Frank's.

My mind flashes back to the dream as I run, being in Tommy's room, the sound of the door shaking in its frame, Stacy screaming, followed by the gunshot.

Everything else is a blur — the neighbors outside looking at me, calling out and asking if everything's okay; Ruby yelling after me; Wilbur sitting on the porch. Nothing matters but getting to Frank's before Tommy does something that he'll regret forever.

I race across the lawn, jump over a broken planter, and run to the front door. I'm about to knock when I hear Stacy scream, "No, don't!"

Instead of knocking, I reach for the doorknob and am surprised to find it unlocked.

I open the door and hear Tommy screaming from his bedroom.

"Let her go!"

I race to the back of the house, see Frank on Tommy's bed, holding a knife to Stacy's throat. Tommy's in the doorway, his gun on Frank.

Tommy turns back, looks up at me, confused. "Mr. Carson?"

Frank says, "What the hell are *you* doing here?"

I ignore him, putting a hand on the boy's shoulder. "It's okay, Tommy, I'm here to help."

His body is shaking, tears streaming from his eyes. "He was hurting her again. I'm sorry."

"It's okay," I say, "Give me the gun."

"No, he's going to kill her."

"No, he won't," I say evaluating the situation. Frank's on the bed, behind Stacy, using her as a shield, holding a butcher knife to her throat. His eyes are red, and I can smell the alcohol from here.

"No, he needs to die," Tommy cries. "I'm tired of him hurting her!"

"You shoot, I kill the bitch," Frank threatens from the bed, glaring at Tommy. "Try me, pussy."

His hand is shaking, finger tightening around the trigger.

I can't let him do this. If he pulls the trigger, his life is over. And there's a damn good chance he'll shoot his mother by accident.

In my calmest voice, I say, "Tommy, don't do this. He's going to kill her if you shoot. Or worse, *you* might shoot your mother."

He shakes his head. "I can't let him get away with this."

"We won't. We'll call the police, have him arrested."

"The hell you will!" Frank says. "Now put the gun down, or I'm gonna cut."

"Shut up!" I shout. "Do you *want* to die?"

He glares at me, disgusted.

"You fuck my woman, then come into *my* house and threaten me?"

"I didn't f— *sleep* with her!" I yell. "It's all a big misunderstanding."

"Then where were you two going?"

"I was trying to help. Stacy and Tommy are scared of you, Frank."

"Bullshit. Your wife said you two were screwing."

"My wife is a crazy bitch," I say, hoping that if I talk in his language, where all women are *bitches*, I might be able to reach him. "Please, put down the knife, and Tommy will drop the gun."

"Yeah, right," Frank says. "I'm not putting down shit until Tommy loses the gun."

Tommy screams, his voice cracking, "Put it down, Frank!"

He's about to blow. If I don't do something, he'll shoot, and Frank isn't doing himself any favors by running his mouth.

I step in front of Tommy, putting myself between them so Tommy can't shoot without hitting me.

"There, Frank, it's safe to put the knife down."

"I wanna see the gun on the floor!"

I turn to Tommy, risking putting my back to Frank.

Tommy looks up at me, eyes uncertain, "What do I do?"

"Put down the gun."

He looks down at the gun then back up to me as if to make sure.

I hear sirens outside. The neighbors called the police. I tell Tommy, "The cops are going to storm in here any second. If they see you with the gun, they'll shoot you, and they might kill your mom in the crossfire. You don't want that to happen, do you? You wanted a way out of this for you and your mom, right? This is the best way you have. But if you shoot Frank, then you throw it all away. You don't want that, do you?"

He shakes his head.

"Then please, put the gun down."

Tommy slowly lowers the gun and places it on the floor.

I turn to Frank. "Let her go."

He looks at Tommy, then up at me. He moves the blade from Stacy's throat.

She leans forward in a rush to get off of the bed and away from him. In my mind, I see him reach up, plunging the blade into her as she's about to escape, laughing through the end of her life.

But he doesn't attack.

Instead, he smiles, that same cocksure grin he gave me earlier as I had to leave with my tail between my legs while Stacy cradled him. That smile that says, "This ain't over; I'll get her back. She'll never leave me."

Stacy is off the bed, hugging Tommy, both of them crying.

I hear police just outside. They'll storm the house any second. Then one of two things will happen. They'll arrest me, they'll arrest Frank, or they'll take both of us and sort things out later at the station.

This fucker can't walk.

I won't allow it.

I turn to Stacy and Tommy. "Go tell the police we're in here."

Stacy looks at me, eyes wide and hopeful, thankful that I intervened, sparing her son. But I think a part of her also knows that this isn't over by a long shot.

She escorts Tommy out.

Frank looks at me, knife in hand, fueling my rage with his fucking smile.

He laughs. "She ain't yours, you know."

"I never said she was. But you and she are done."

"I don't think so, partner. You see, me and her got something you can't understand. The kind of love that lasts forever. And ain't no faggy teacher gonna take her away."

I look down at Tommy's gun on the ground.

Frank follows my eyes.

His nostrils flare, his body tenses, his fist tightens around the blade.

I drop to the ground and raise the gun.

He's off the bed and coming right at me, blade arcing, inches from my gut.

I fall back, aiming as I do, and blast Frank four times in the chest.

He stumbles back, but then hurls himself forward. Momentum takes him straight into me, knocking me back.

His body on top of me, wild eyes glaring at me, I blast twice more until I'm certain that he's dead.

I shove him off of me and get to my feet, gun still on him, half expecting him to make one final lunge.

Behind me, I hear the boom of a man's voice.

"Drop the gun! Hands on your head."

I follow the officer's orders.

The cop wrestles my hands from my head to behind my back, then cuffs me.

I don't resist.

I stare at Frank, lying on his back, face up, wide-open eyes staring up at the ceiling. I watch the blood pool beneath him. I watch his eyes to make sure they don't move, to make sure he's dead.

To make sure this is over.

Finally, it is.

Epilogue

Epilogue

I WAKE up far from Baker Street.

Today my name is Bo Jackson, a 21-year-old DJ. It's eight in the morning, and I'm glad to wake up alone in his apartment.

I go to his computer and do a news search for any information on Stacy, Tommy, and Craig. So far, there are not many details. Frank was dead on the scene. Both Stacy and her child, not named in the articles due to his age, were safe. Craig's situation was still up in the air with "charges pending."

I'm hoping that means he'll get off, that it'll be obvious that he shot Frank in self-defense. Things will get murky when you factor in that Craig had had a fight with the victim just hours earlier and had gone to Ruby's house asking for a gun. Also, Tommy's situation could get dicey if police find out that *he* took Ruby's gun.

But at least they're all alive, and Frank is dead. Not the happiest of endings, but better than the ones that seemed destined to play out. Hopefully better than whatever the assassin said would happen if Frank didn't die.

Bo's cell phone buzzes.

I pick it up, look at the screen to see the name Jinx, along with a picture of a blue-haired girl with a small butterfly henna tattoo on her cheek — his girlfriend, and a text:

Can you pick up some soy milk and organic grapes before you pick me up?

Bo's mind fills me in on the details. He is supposed to pick Jinx up and drive her to the garage to get her car, which needed a new transmission.

Okay, I text back.

I shower, throw on some blue jeans and a gray T-shirt, and head out the door.

I DRIVE to the closest grocery store, searching the cooler for a soy milk that I see in Bo's memories. I find it, then head over to the produce section. There are several bags of grapes on display, but none that specifically say organic.

I look around for someone to help me, find a short guy pushing a cart of produce through double doors into the back of the store.

I try to call out to him, but he doesn't hear me as he disappears through the double doors.

I wait for him, or another employee, so I can ask for help. It's funny how you can never find help in a store when you need it. So many times, in so many different bodies, I've been accosted by salespeople, "Can I help you?" the second I walked into a store, before I've even had a chance to browse. But the moment I *need* help finding something, the employees vanish like ghosts.

The double doors open, and the man resurfaces, pushing a cart filled with boxes of bananas.

"Excuse me," I say, "do you carry organic grapes?"

The guy looks over to where I'd been looking, then says, "What kind you looking for?"

I'm not sure. Jinx didn't specify, and I'm not getting any grape-related memories from Bo.

"Red?"

"Okay, lemme check the back," the guy says as he leaves the cart next to the double doors, then returns to the stock room.

I watch as a young couple pushes their cart into the produce section. They stick out because they're both wearing tight workout clothes that accentuate bodies built through sweat and great genes. They're arguing about something, but I'm too far away to hear. The guy, wearing a baseball cap to hide seemingly thinning hair, is bitching about something, his hands moving frantically as he tries to understand why the woman is so unreasonable. "It's not for you to decide," the woman says, not even looking at him, her attention on her phone. I wonder if she's doing that to annoy him further. If so, it's working.

He looks like he's on the verge of violence, though maybe not, as he's doing a pretty good job of keeping his voice down. Usually, people prone to violent outbursts in public aren't all that concerned about lowering their voice.

Suddenly, another sound has my attention, though — static.

And a woman's voice saying something inaudible.

I look around, trying to see where the sound might be coming from.

But then I realize it's just like that broadcast I heard in the parking lot just before I first saw the assassin.

I look around for any sign of the assassin, not that I'd know what body he or she will show up in this time.

Is that why I'm here? To prevent another murder, or perhaps screw up something again?

The broadcast gets a bit louder as if I'm getting closer to the source of the signal.

"Wearing blue jeans and a gray shirt. No weapon."

I look around for someone wearing blue jeans and a gray shirt.

I'm the only one.

Shit. Am I *a target?*

There are only three other people in the produce section: the arguing couple and an old lady who is hunched over the melon section testing each and every one, it seems, to find the perfect fruit.

Suddenly, another person steps into the produce section, a Latin girl in her twenties, with bright pink cotton candy-colored hair, wearing shades, blue jeans, and a sky-blue shirt.

She's making a beeline right at me.

Her hand is in her purse.

Oh, shit.

I try not to panic. Try to tell myself she's just looking for squash or something, but no, she is passing all the fruit and veggies, heading toward the rear of the store where I'm standing.

I don't know what to do.

I look around for something I can use as a weapon but come up empty. I doubt even a ninja could put a box of bananas to use in self-defense.

Even though I'm in someone else's body, and I don't think *I* can be harmed even if my host is killed, the fight-or-flight response is always there.

And right now it's telling me to run away — fast.

She's twenty feet away.

I want to run, but I'm frozen in place.

I can't understand why my host's body is refusing to cooperate with my instruction to get the hell out of here.

Pink Hair reaches me, removes her glasses.

I see the flash of blue light in her eyes, just barely there, and then gone.

"You've got to get out of here," she says, keeping her voice low.

"Why?" I ask, relieved she doesn't seem like she's going to kill me, but anxious to know why she's here, and why she's telling me to flee.

"They're here."

"Who?"

"The Collectors."

"Who are *The Collectors?*"

"No time to explain, Ella. But you need to go, or they *will* eat your soul."

She knows my name. Is this the assassin from before? Or ... another one?

"*Eat my soul?* What? How?" I say, trying to pull reason from her words.

The confirmation that I, the person jumping between hosts, can die sends a chill to my core.

Suddenly, a loud crash, someone dropping something.

I turn to see the blonde fitness freak standing over her phone lying broken on the ground.

She's staring at it blankly as if struggling to figure out how it got there.

As I try to determine whether or not her boyfriend snapped and knocked the phone from her, another realization dawns on me.

She's no longer looking at the phone.

She's looking at me.

As is her boyfriend.

Their faces suddenly *flicker*. For a moment, it's their

faces. But then, for just a second, I see something else — almost a blank face, as if the details of their faces were sanded down.

Then their faces are normal again — except the vacant stares.

What the hell is happening?

They begin walking toward us, vacant stares marred only by the slightest flash of white light in their eyes.

"Go!" Pink Hair yells, pulling out a gun and firing at the male fitness freak.

Two shots hit him, but he keeps coming.

I turn to run along the rear aisle along the back of the store, then stop dead in my tracks when I see two more people with flickering faces — a stock man in a blue apron and an old black man clutching a cane, blocking my escape. They have the same vacant look in their eyes — almost like marionettes being controlled by someone or something.

The stock man grabs me before I can react.

I kick and thrash, trying to break free, but his grip is like a vice.

As he holds me, the old man approaches, his mouth open impossibly wide, as if his jaw were unhinged.

Behind me, I hear Pink Hair shooting: one, two, three shots.

Are there more Collectors, or is she just shooting the same ones and not doing any damage?

Suddenly, a terrible shrieking sound screams from the old man's gaping maw as he comes closer.

I can't move. The stock man's grip is almost supernaturally strong.

But there's something else. I find myself struggling to move at all, transfixed, staring into the old man's wide open mouth.

I can feel a part of myself being sucked out of my host and toward the old man's mouth — as if it were some horrible soul-sucking vacuum.

And in a sickening instant, I realize that Pink Hair was speaking literally when she said that The Collectors were here to eat my soul.

I cry out, straining to turn my gaze away from the old man Collector and his wide-open mouth and its terrible shriek that sounds like the end of the universe.

Pink Hair turns and sees the situation I'm in.

"Help!" I scream.

She runs toward us.

But instead of shooting the Collectors, she brings the gun to my head, "Sorry, this is the only way."

She pulls the trigger.

I WAKE, in another body.

Safe.

But for how long?

A Quick Favor...

____

If you enjoyed this book, please take a moment to write a short review on your favorite online bookstore so other readers can enjoy it, too.

Thanks so much!

About the Authors

Sean Platt is an entrepreneur and founder of Sterling & Stone, where he makes stories with his partners, Johnny B. Truant, and David W. Wright, and a family of storytellers.

Sean is the bestselling author of over 10 million words' worth of books, including the Yesterday's Gone and Invasion series. Sean is also co-author of the indie publishing cornerstone, Write. Publish. Repeat. and co-host of the Story Studio Podcast.

Originally from Long Beach, California, Sean now lives in Austin, Texas with his wife and two children. He has more than his share of nose.

David W. Wright is the co-author of edge-of-your seat thrillers including the best-selling post-apocalyptic series *Yesterday's Gone*, the paranoid sci-fi *WhiteSpace* series, and the vigilante series, *No Justice*, as well as standalone thrillers *12*, and *Crash* which was recently optioned for a movie.

David is an accomplished, though intermittent, cartoonist who lives in [LOCATION REDACTED] with his wife and son [NAMES REDACTED.]

He is not at all paranoid.

He is "the grumpy one" on the *The Story Studio Podcast* with fellow Sterling and Stone founders, Sean Platt and Johnny B. Truant.

David writes about books, TV shows, movies, and

video games he enjoys; his struggles with anxiety and OCD; writing; and posts the occasional drawing at his personal blog at davidwwright.com

You can email him at david@sterlingandstone.net

We swear, he almost never bites. Unless you feed him after midnight.

For a full list of his most recent books visit sterlingand-stone.net.

Also By Sean Platt

The Dead World Series

Dead Zero

Dead City

Dead Nation

Dead Planet

Empty Nest

The Beam Series

The Beam Season One

The Beam Season Two

The Beam Season Three

Robot Proletariat Series

En3my

Robot Proletariat

The Infinite Loop

The Hard Reset

Cascade Failure

Reboot

The Tomorrow Gene Series

Null Identity

The Tomorrow Gene

The Tomorrow Clone

The Eden Experiment

Karma Police Series

Jumper

Karma Police

The Collectors

Deviant

The Fall

Homecoming

Yesterday's Gone

October's Gone

Yesterday's Gone Season One

Yesterday's Gone Season Two

Yesterday's Gone Season Three

Yesterday's Gone Season Four

Yesterday's Gone Season Five

Yesterday's Gone Season Six

Tomorrow's Gone

Tomorrow's Gone Season One

Tomorrow's Gone Season Two

Tomorrow's Gone Season Three

Available Darkness

Darkness Itself

Available Darkness Book One

Available Darkness Book Two

Available Darkness Book Three

WhiteSpace

WhiteSpace Season One

WhiteSpace Season Two

WhiteSpace Season Three

Stand Alone Novels

Burnout

The Island

Crash

Emily's List

Pattern Black

Devil May Care

The Secret Within

Also By David W. Wright

Cold Vengeance

Cold Vengeance

Cold Reckoning

Hidden Justice

Hidden Justice

Hidden Honor

Hidden Shame

Hidden Virtue

No Justice

No Justice

No Escape

No Hope

No Return

No Stopping

No Fear

Karma Police

Jumper

Karma Police

The Collectors

Deviant

The Fall

Homecoming

Yesterday's Gone

October's Gone

Yesterday's Gone Season One

Yesterday's Gone Season Two

Yesterday's Gone Season Three

Yesterday's Gone Season Four

Yesterday's Gone Season Five

Yesterday's Gone Season Six

Tomorrow's Gone

Tomorrow's Gone Season One

Tomorrow's Gone Season Two

Tomorrow's Gone Season Three

Available Darkness

Darkness Itself

Available Darkness Book One

Available Darkness Book Two

Available Darkness Book Three

WhiteSpace

WhiteSpace Season One

WhiteSpace Season Two

WhiteSpace Season Three

Stand Alone Novels

Crash

Emily's List

Threshold

The Secret Within